THE DIAMOND FAMILY

Loyalty, Betrayal, Revenge

VANETTA MASON

ISBN: 978-1-957956-95-4 (sc)
ISBN: 978-1-957956-96-1 (e)

Rev. date: 03/22/2023

CHAPTER 1
The Funeral

I can't believe she's gone sister, Janelle says to her sister Harper crying.

Harper puts her arms around her little sister, for whom for years she played more of a mother to than our real mother.

I know, let's just get through this funeral and deal with the rest later.

Sis, who the hell are those fools in the white and red suits? I have no idea, but, i'm about to find out!

Janelle and I were the two oldest so we were always on guard of Mother always. As we stand at the door all the guests arrive and people are coming up to us to say how sorry they are, yeah right most of you people feared my Mother and so I know your offer of condolences are empty. Most of these people couldn't care less about my Mother! The FEDS were in attendance too. They had to make their presence known I guess. I had no problem with them being there either, they had been in our lives since we were children, we knew exactly how to deal with their asses. We decided to have the funeral at the Mormon Temple in the Oakland Hills. We weren't Mormon's or anything but, I know Mother came here sometimes to clear her head. She always said it was such a beautiful place, plus, we buried Mother in her Armani coke white suit and her white Ferragamo heels with her beautiful white mink coat, she was laid to rest in a gold encrusted glass coffin and it was to be led by White Arabian Horses down Skyline Blvd just so Mother could get one last look at the city skyline she loved so much and at the end we released a dozen doves into a beautiful evening sky with colors of orange, pink, and amazing purples, it was a truly spectacular sight.

Well, how rude of me not to give a proper introduction, my name is Harper Diamond, huh, with a name like that you would've thought we were royalty.

In a way, we kinda were. I have two sisters named Janelle Diamond and Skye Diamond. We are the daughters of the biggest drug Queenpin in Northern California. Our Mother Jackie Diamond was a force to be reckoned with. Mother comes from "old money", what that means is Mother, Mother family has been a staple in California since the late 1800's. The Diamond family has owned most of the West Coast for centuries. Mother has so much property and assets it's ridiculous. Mother's parents were the cream of the crop! High society, and very well educated. When Mother came to be 18 years old she decided that she was tired of being stuck in old tradition and wanted to make her own mark. And, that she did. My Mother had everything anyone could want, but it was all about how she was able to utilize it. The Diamond Family already had prestige and clout, I mean there's not any high official or law enforcement to judges, everyone was taken care of so that Mother could move how she wanted to without disgracing the family name. After Mother became successful and came more into her own empire, she shined, like a newly polished diamond. Mother always made sure that when she became pregnant with me, she would do whatever it takes to raise us with the best education and totally lethal!! Mother has had things in position for us since our births, there is an envelope for each of us in the horrible case of her demise to keep things rolling and to make sure we never work for anyone and can always be successful. Harper completely understood that now that her Mother was gone the Diamond family is now a target and in danger of insider betrayal.

Someone got some courage or one of our enemies grew some balls and ended my Mother's life. Either way, I will find out!!

Mother was murdered a week ago in a drug deal gone wrong, So we were told, somewhere in Houston,Texas.

The funeral arrangements are really nice Harp! Janelle said looking at her sister, she was the only one who called me that, ever since we were kids. Thank you, it was really hard to decide on what to do, we knew we wanted it to be extravagant and a big special gathering.

Mother looks so beautiful in the glass coffin we picked out for her. I couldn't decide on which flowers of mother's favorites I should use, you know.

I just decided on Casablanca Lilies, they are elegant like Mother. Anyway, how are you doing?

I'm fine sister, I know I'm the baby but I got this.

Skye, you know you don't need to be drinking!, Harper says to her sister with irritation in her voice.

I always looked after my sisters, that's the duty of being the oldest. Skye is the baby of the family, 29 and every bit of it, ok!!

She gives me migraines this one, she is so out of control sometimes.

The funeral was coming to a close and everybody lined up to say how sorry they were and some people even told their own personal stories with our Mother and some left gifts and cards and even flowers. As the people started to leave the church my sisters and I were talking in the hallway and three men walked up to us and asked us if we were Jackie's girls?

We all looked at each other with the same question in each of our heads.. Skye, who had too much to drink by this time, said loudly..

Hell yeah, who wants to know?

The men just looked at us and smiled and said good to know, sorry to hear about your mother, She was a very lovely woman.

He extended his hand out as if to ask for a handshake, nigga please!

Skye said with a crazy laugh.

Ain't y'all a long way from home anyway?

It was very easy to tell they were from out of town by the way they look, there are other tell signs but these niggas obviously wanted to be seen and what I call Noisey!

Best be getting back to your side of the state line my brothers!!

After that little exchange me and the girls got into the Bentley limo that would follow the coffin down Skyline blvd.

You can see people lining up in their cleanest whips to follow the funeral procession. It was beautiful!

Afterwards, everyone started to head up to Mother's Mansion in the Oakland Hills.

As the oldest daughter I think I need to call a meeting and get everyone together. Make sure everyone is on point and knows their position.

Once we arrived at the house I had the staff decorate so when you pulled up all you saw was Elegance!!

When we got out of the car the valet men were taking peoples cars and parking them and the staff were ushering people to where they needed to be.

Harp!

What Up?

I need to make a run real quick.

What? Skye, what the hell are you talking about? This is not the time for you to go off on one of your "runs"!

Shit girl, I gotta a few moves I gotta make right quick, you got this! I'll be right back sis!! She says as she's laughing and stumbling in my Gucci pumps as she gets into the car. Take the limo Skye, please don't drive!!

Ok, for you Harp, Anything for you baby. Drunk ass, that one boy!! Whew...

The house was full of people who knew our mother and those who wanted to. We decided to have the repass at mother's mansion in the Oakland hills.

She really loved it here.

As Harper and Janelle say their goodbyes to the guest,Then, I spot Dante'. This was my mom's right hand man, I definitely need to talk to him.

Hey yo Dante'?

Oh, hey lil sis. How are you holding up?

Getting through, you know me, staying busy. What about you?

I'm fine. I guess, I just can't believe she is really gone. I'm already on that too. As I knew you would be, you weren't her right hand for nothing. Ok !!

I'll be fine once we get past all this.

You'll be fine regardless girl, you always got it together.

I felt his hand come around the small of my back to embrace me but I stopped him in mid-hug, No, won't be going down that road again.

Can't deny it was really nice!

Yes, but it's in the past and right now there's work to do. You're right Boss.

What did you just call me?

I called you Boss, Oh you mean to tell me it hasn't crossed your mind that someone needs to take her position, right?

Been so busy with the funeral and flying guests out here and shit that it hadn't occurred to me.

I'll hit you later Dante' to talk more about business. Cool, wait to hear from you.Peace.

As I'm walking D to the door I hear Skye pulling up, loud ass. I told you I'd be right back sister, Janelle, where are you baby?

My Mother would kill me if she knew that I was hollering in her house I'm in the office, here I come.

Meet us in the back office, we need to talk. Ok.

The back office is sound proof and is swept for bugs daily, so it's where we talk freely and openly.

Alright sisters, Mother built this shit from the mother-fuckin ground up and I'll be damned if anyone is gonna just take it!!

So what needs to happen now is who is willing to take care of what?

Good thing Mother taught us the business just in case we ever needed to make some change, we knew what to do.

What do you think Harper? Just tell us who should do what. ok, Well, I think Skye should take care of all enforcement duties, Janelle, you handle the connect and I will deal with the money. Sounds cool to everybody?

Damn, Harper, you've been giving this some thought huh? Said Skye.

No, not really but mother did sit me down a couple of years ago to tell me what and how she thought we should do things"!

Mother was such a real chick, you know?

She never fucked no body out of their money or did nothing wrong to other people, at least none that didn't deserve it.

The girls and I all have a good laugh on that one.

As I think about her I hope she is looking down and is proud of how everything went. Harper replied with an attitude.

"Come on you guys we need to stick together more than anything now right?" says Janelle.

"You are right sis we got it.

All of them came together in the middle of the office and just held on to each other. "This is just the beginning ladies, we're going to take over shit!! After the house was cleared of the guests, Harper went and paid all the staff and the girls turned in for the night. All night Harper was in her room stirring, trying to figure out who?, what? When? How? And why?!!! She sits down on her bed and weeps. As she lays down she realizes that at that moment she became that little girl that wanted to be just like her Mother, until she grew up and learned about life. Mother never changed our rooms from when we lived here with her.

The next day the girls got up for breakfast after spending the night at mother's house, it made them feel close to her.

"Good morning sister" "what up nigga" ha, ha. I'm just playing sis good morning boo" Skye you so stupid.

The sisters share a laugh while waiting for Janelle to join them. "I'm gonna need you to go and handle some shit out in Antioch for me, Cool what up?

Some dumb mothafucka is trying to take something that does not belong to them!! And, they need their hand spanked ok boo!!

"It's about time, chick" teased Harper.

I know taking all that time girl, ain't nobody about to be waiting all day for yo ass ok? "Shut up Skye.

I miss anything? Says Janelle.

No it's cool sis" Harper says calmly. Eat up ladies we got work to do.

The girls then finished their meals and began getting ready to tackle the day. There were some rumors floating around about mother's death but, we will get to the bottom of it fo sho!

My mother's name was Jackie, she was the life of the party and the boss lady on the streets. People respected her whether they knew her or not. She helped the community as well as I guess destroy it but, we gotta fight to sustain this empire for our families. Harper began to drive up the coast to clear her head a little when her phone began to ring.

"Hello

"Hey,bitch I got some tea for your ass! " What crazy?

"I just found out that the muthafuckas in Houston sent some niggas up here for mother! "WHAT?

"Yes bitch, Houston. "Ready to take a ride? Skye asks her sister, already knowing the response.

"Hell yeah bitch, let's do it!" says Harper.

Harper knows what "take a ride" means when her sister says that. We about to go merk these niggas!

Janelle calls and they all meet up later at their favorite lounge called The Spot. The sisters walk in and all eyes are on them, muthafuckas staring so hard and trying to figure out a way into these jeans, never!

We sat down at our usual table, in the back but with a clear view of the door.

Janelle asks" So, what's up ladies?

Well y'all know I got the club down in Miami? Yeah we both replied at the same time, wait, you still got that strip club sis? How is that shit going down there?

"Off the fuckin chain girl, you going to have to down let yo lil sis hook you up one time!! yeah we'll see about that baby girl" Anyway what's the tea?

As Janelle was asking the question I was running through my head about how mother sounded when she called to check on me last month, she sounded worried and like something was bothering her. I swear I will get to the bottom of this if it's the last thing I do! "Skye told me that she heard it was some fools from Houston that did our mother "WHAT!!

" Yes sis, but you know what time it is now right? Harper asks her sister. "Hell yeah, it's merk a nigga time.

The girls headed out the club later that evening, after seeing a few people and watching the business. Neither of us sisters was looking forward to doing what needed to be done, but instead of sending a crew it had to be us! After making sure my sisters were straight for the night, I began to think about our lives before all this madness.

We each have businesses of our own and how are we going to run this shit and them?

CHAPTER 2

Harper Diamond

I am the oldest of three girls. There's me Harper and I am 40. I own my own business. I have several homes dedicated to taking care of children with Autism. I live in Castro Valley.

I have locations of my business in Atlanta, San Francisco, and Los Angeles. I am very successful as all of us are. I have my master's degree in child psychology and business entrepreneurship. Before hearing the awful news about my mother's death, I was in the process of branching out to try some new ventures. I am not married and have no children. My biological clock is ticking so damn loud, fucker keeps me up some nights. I'm just not ready for a marriage right now but, that doesn't mean a bitch don't be getting it in when needed! Ok! There are some cutie pies that I spend some time with but nothing serious. Yet!

I have someone special but I'm not ready for what he's ready for

Sincere, whew!! Every bit of fine as hell and a body that won't quit. He's a very nice distraction but I have always been about my coins!!

I need to talk to my sisters and make sure everyone is on the same page on what to do next. Suddenly, Harper hears her favorite song coming from her purse, speaking of gettin it in, here go my boo thang now calling. " Hey baby, How are you doing, sweetheart?

" I'm fine, babe.

"Can I come over to sit with you, I know you tough and shit but, your mom just died man, you need someone.

"You're right, I could use the company" "Thank you boo, see you soon. I'll call you when I get to the house.

Sounds good baby, I'll be waiting.

Now, look at that, speak on a nigga and they call.

Sincere. He is what it sounds like, he's a sweetie. The thing is though, no one knew about who my Mother was and what she did. I kept that part of my life separate from anything that I was doing. It's gonna be kinda hard lying to him about things but no one can know what our plan is!

Trust No One! Mother always said,

I wonder which one of her rules did she break to get herself killed!! That's ok cause we'll find out who did what soon enough.

Let me call Sincere back, "Hi sweetie

"Hey girl, what's up? Are you home yet?" replies Sincere stretching while answering her.

Yes, just walked in babe. "I'm on my way shawty!

I laid out some nice lingerie and before I was able to get out of the tub, he was standing in my bathroom naked in the doorway, holding sliced pineapple and watermelon!

"Coming, " I said to him. "I always do!

He sits the fruit down on the counter and steps into the tub. As he is lowering his beautiful, caramel coated, sculpted body down in the water his eyes never left mine. How are you my love?

I'm fine now, miss me?

Let me show you baby, come here.

Sincere grabs Harper around her waist and ass and pulls her close to him, wrapping her legs around him and begins kissing her with such passion and strength. He stands up with her in arms and inserts himself inside her. Harper wraps her long legs around his waist and begins to squeeze tighter so she can get enough grip on him to ride him like never before.

She gets down and pulls Sincere into the bedroom and he walks up behind her and grabs her by the hair and takes her from the back. Every time he moves in and out of her there is a feeling of pure ecstacy with every thrust. Then he turns her around to pick her up again and gently lays her down on the bed and wraps both of her legs around him and starts making passionate love to Harper. It's exactly what she needs right now. Someone to give her an escape for a little while, and what better way to escape than in the arms of a man who truly loves you. Especially after Julian Green.

What a terrible man. He abused her in every way, used her and took advantage of her love for him and the fact that she would do anything for him, he ruined her for a while. Took poor Harper a year in a half to get over Julian. But, some men come to tear down, and some come to restore or rebuild. So to say the least, when I met Sincere at the coffee house in Miami I knew he was one who restores. After all of that love making, Sincere and I laid in each other's arms and fell asleep talking. He is my best friend. He is always there when I need him, even when I don't know I need him.

The next morning, I called Skye to see when we were moving and what the get down was going to be?

" Hey sis, how are you doing this morning?"

I'm ok Skye just trying to figure out where did mother go wrong? you know she would never drop any of her rules for nobody.

"Somebody got close, "When was the last time you spoke to mother Skye? "Girl, it had to be a couple of months ago at least.

"Did she sound funny to you at all?

"No, she sounded like mother, bossy as hell. And trying to tell me how to run my business, the usual!

"Ok, call Janelle and meet me at mother's house, meet you in about an hour "Cool Bet!".

Sweetheart, I need to get up and handle some business, so I'm gonna hop in the shower and get dressed, you can let yourself out.

She kissed him on his forehead and went into the bathroom. While Harper is in the shower Sincere got dressed and went downstairs to the kitchen and put on some coffee for her. He was always so considerate like that. He left a note on the counter saying, had fun as usual, love you.

I'm very patient baby!

Understand you, more than you know. Sin.

Harper comes downstairs and sees that Sin left a note and made her some coffee, he has always been sweet like that. I'm gonna have to have a conversation with him one day to reel in whatever this is we're doing. He has been very patient.

CHAPTER 3
Skye Diamond

Now, my sister Skye is no joke. She has always been a little knuckle-head since we were kids. She is 28 and lives out in Los Angeles. She owns and runs 3 strip clubs, one in Miami,FL., one in Vegas,NV and one in Atlanta, Ga.

She has her bachelor's degree in Psychology and Business management. She used to be a dancer before she realized shit, I can do this shit myself! Skye loves the finer things in life, so she is always traveling. She doesn't have any children either, but doesn't want any right now. She does really well for herself as an entrepreneur. I am so proud of her, and I know Janelle is too.

Skye pulls up to her residence to find her home has been ransacked. Not much from what she could see was missing. She calls the cops, they come to investigate the break in and told her they would contact her if they find out anything, and that she should do the same. These poor cops don't know my sister at all, she will find out who did this! We stay out of the limelight on purpose just like our dear Mother taught us.

Even though no one has seen us do any dealings on the street, they do know what we are capable of!!

"Now, as the youngest sister, I'm in charge of enforcing all the businesses. So whoever did this I think is trying to send a message of some sort. Oh well, that's not gonna stop us from finding out anything we want to know, the streets are talking baby, and my ear is to the ground!! Skye reaches in her purse to retrieve her phone,

"Hello, this Skye, round em up Nate, shit just got real "Meet me down by the port of oakland at 11:00pm, wait for further instructions! As the housekeeper is cleaning up the terrible mess left behind by the break in, Skye calls her sisters to let them know what the hell is going on. " Hello"

"Harp you sleep?

"It's good sis what's wrong?" she replies sleepy.

Some muthafuckas just broke into my fuckin house bitch, and I think it's got something to do with Mother!"

"I'm on my way sis!" "No, I'm gonna meet up with the crew to see what the streets is saying about all this.

"Ok, you call Big Nate?"

"yep, sis I just wanted you to know what was going on, call Janelle to make sure she cool and I will get back wit you later.

"Cool sis, love you and stay safe ok bye.

CHAPTER 4
Janelle Diamond

My sister Janelle is the middle sister and crazy as hell. She lives out in Pacifica, Ca. real close to the bay area. She likes that big money shit. Looking over the ocean type shit. She has her master's degree in Psychology and business/contract law. She also doesn't have any children yet, she is 36 years old and has a fabulous life. She has a few businesses too.

She owns two cell phone stores and a couple of Tanning Salons. Janelle deals with the connect part of this plan, she has dealt with this before so she is well versed in the subject. One of her tanning salons is in the Bayfair Mall in San Leandro, Ca. and the other is in Monterey, Ca. both very successful.

As she pulled up to her one mile driveway through some iron gate and reached her front door, she noticed that her door was wide open. Well she knew something was wrong because her cleaning crew was given the night off. She slowly approached the house and began calling 911 on her cell phone as she peeked in.

" Hello, officer, there has been a breakin at my home, come quickly!

The police are on their way now and all Janelle can think of is that this just happened to Skye?

What's up? "Someone knows something, someone is close!!

She calls her sisters on three-way and all three of them begin to figure out who is trying them at this point. Time to narrow down the suspects.

"Let's meet right now where we used to play as kids, "Kennedy park?" asks Janelle.

"Yes," says Harper.

If this is happening to you guys, I'm next! "Ok meet you in twenty minutes sisters, love!

Janelle goes in to check on her safe and it was still intact but she found a cell phone that wasn't hers. One of them fools must have dropped it on his way out. So, Janelle takes the phone to meet with her sisters to show them what she found and to figure out who is doing this to them.

As the girls arrive at the park it's dark and secluded like they thought it would be, except for a black charger with dark tinted windows. We all parked close to one another and to keep an eye on that car.

"Can anybody tell me what's going on?

Look Mother is gone and now muthafuckas want her territory.

Now that we're here we need to decide if we want to do this or close up shop for good! Cause once we start this, it's on!

"I say let's do it! laughed Skye.

"Fuck it, it ain't like Mother didn't lace us cause she did. So, let's take care of our own company's and jump into this shit so we can actually find out the Who and the Why? "All in agreement?" asks Harper as she can see the looks on her sisters faces.

"Hell yeah, let's do it" says Skye.

"You good Janelle? Cause if you don't want to get involved let us know baby? "Bitch, pass the blunt and let's do this shit!!

CHAPTER 5

So, the girls go to their houses to pack for this trip they were about to take that's going to change everything!

Harper got on the phone and calls some of the dudes that worked for Mother to see if anyone could throw some names our way. I already know Dante' is down for whatever, I just wanted some unfamiliar faces.

When I talked to Dante', now this was Mother's right hand man, if anybody would know something it would be him. Plus, at the funeral he pulled me to the side to tell me he had some business to discuss with me. So I figured I would make that call now.

Yo, D, what's up wit you?

Shit, out here doing it, what about you? Any closer to what we talked about?

Actually yes I am, I want some more goons with blank faces, you know? Right, right, makes sense to be cautious Boss.

Chill with the Boss shit D, Mother is still the Boss.

Girl, wake up and look at what's happening around you, your Mother knew out of the three of you which one will carry the crown. That's you boo!!

Feel you D. you're right too. So I'm gonna need you to get me some Blanks ASAP!!

I got Boss Lady!! Harp! Just fucking wit you.

You so damn crazy, so what did you want to discuss that you pulled to the side at the funeral to tell me you got tea, Spill!!

Oh, I do.

Dante' explained to me that he overheard a conversation my Mother was having with some new connect in Houston. His name was Big E. He wanted to work with her on an expansion deal, but she did not want to deal with Texas and their strict ass laws. Dude seemed very pissed off that this deal wasn't going to happen and began making threats, well, you know we don't do threats!! So, Mother sent me down to talk to the nigga see where his head is and to let him know Mother was not to be fucked with. Period. "So, what if anything came from your trip down south?

"It was real informative.

" Ok cool, I'm meeting up with the girls soon and we all need to talk, they need to hear this as well.

I'm going to call you in about 40 minutes, I'll tell you from there". "Bet!"

Harper continues to pack her shit but, she starts to think about what D said and it got her making plans for this "Big E"!!

The sisters show up at one of the most expensive restaurants in the city. As they walked in with the finest of everything from Gucci to Louis V. on their backs, everyone's eyes were on these ladies, as if they were stars! They told Maitre D to sit them near the window, but in the back of the restaurant.

"Mother always told us to sit with our backs to the wall so you can see the door!" remembers Skye.

" So what's up big sis, what's the plan of action?" says Janelle.

"I wanted to wait until we got here before I tell y'all, I called D to get some info about anything Mother might have been working on? Or anyone new she may have been talking to?

"What did D say sis?" asks Skye.

"D told me that he overheard Mother talking to this dude on the phone, he was trying to set up a distribution deal and something about expanding?"

Harper looked at the looks on her sisters faces and she knew they weren't with the bullshit!

What the fuck were we going to do about this shit? " so I asked him to meet us here, he can answer the rest of our questions plus, I want him to roll with us since he seen the nigga.

"What, D know what the nigga look like and every?" Janelle says surprised. "hell yeah, bitch" Harper replies, cutting Janelle off.

"Now, you know mother had D go down there and check this nigga's pulse cause from what I understand there were threats being made?"

"Ain't no way in hell is Mother gonna take no country ass nigga talking shit to her!" Skye says with an attitude.

Your right sister.

"Hey Dante', Have a seat handsome" Skye says, directing Dante' to sit next to her.

she always had a thing for him. He always looked at her as if but, he was told to look at us like sisters to him though.

Dante' begins to fill the sisters in on everything that transpired between our Mother and this clown "Big E". Dante' knew all about this man and his comings and goings daily. "Beautiful all we need now is to get this shit poppin" Yells Harper to her sisters as they high five each other.

CHAPTER 6

The sisters and Dante' arrive at the Bush airport in Houston, Texas and the heat smacks them in the face as they deboard the plane.

" Hot enough for you D?" asks Skye bending over to pick up her luggage.

"You are so damn stupid girl" Janelle says, laughing at Skye shamelessly flirting with Dante'.

He trying his best to be good, but she makes it damn near impossible for the man.

"Hey ya'll, cut it out, we here on business," says Harper. The town car pulls up and we hop in.

"Ooh yeah air condition, it's hot as shit out there" Skye says as she puts her face directly in front of the vent.

"Sir, we're going to the Plaza Hotel, thank you" Harper tells the driver.

Of course ma'am" replies the driver.

We get to the hotel and get our rooms, "everyone meet in my room in an hour!" Harper tells everybody.

As they all get situated, Harper and Dante' go over the fire power and the plan to get this pussy out in the open!

"You hook up with your people's out here yet?" Harper asks him. "Yep, everything's set, they're just waiting on the call.

Cool, let them know it's tonight so be on point.

I got it Sis, this ain't exactly my first rodeo you know?

I do know, just I move just slightly a bit more stealth than Mother. Right Boss.

The sisters show up to Harper room just as requested, and the plan is called into action.

"So, D says the nigga is stuck at the strip club all day all night on fridays, D got a bitch that work the club and going to let us know when he goes in the back for that private dance.

Suddenly, D's phone rings and it's shawty with the trap. What up?

It's me nigga.

I know bitch, he's there?

Yep, waiting on a lap dance from yours truly.

Good stall his ass for about 30 minutes, we are on the way. Alright, I will be waiting.

Bet.

So the bitch said he's ready now. It's time to jet.

"Cool, let's hit it." Harper and her sisters leave the hotel dressed to impress, but ready to kill!!

They pull up to the club and go in like superstars. Everyone wants to know who the hell is these women are? We look every bit of confidence, money and power! Dante' spots the muthafucka in the corner with a bunch of bitches around him.

We grab a booth in the back but in perfect view of the target. As the waitress comes over I ask for the baddest bitch in the place to come over and dance, then, I ask for the money gun, and shoot ten racks in the air real quick to get their attention.

It worked because in 2.2 seconds the target was sending over a bottle of the finest champagne. Skye looks at me and I give her the ok to get the cyanide pill and give it to the stripper.

I picked the baddest bitch they had, and I sent our friend Big E a very expensive lap dance. His very last lap dance. The stripper I sent to him walked him to the back, she was Dante's friend Pleasure.

She looked the part and all, I had to make sure she was bad because i needed her to be able to get real close to the nigga. We continued to party in the front of the club, Dante' kept an eye on the "work" while us girls had fun!! I looked at the clock around 1:30am and shawty was coming out of the back room, alone. Dante' brought her to me.

"You do your fuckin job ho?" I politely asked her. "Yes I did, he came and then he went!!"

"Just how I like it clean and quiet" Harper says to Pleasure, "Let's go sisters, we got a plane to catch."

"Dante take care of our new friend." " Fo sho sis!" he responds.

Alright D see you in the Bay nigga." Skye yells at Dante'. "Not if I see you first, boo!"

We leave the club with a weight lifted off of us. We got one of the muthafuckas that had something to do with Mother's death. We all know that wasn't a one man show, she was too big!

We boarded the plane and was out of Houston on the red eye back to Cali. I don't really know how I feel about what we just did, it had been weighing on me during the flight. My sisters on the other hand are great. I guess because I'm the oldest I look at things from Mother's point of view. It was the only view for a long time, but now things are different. Like for instance, Mother would have killed him in front of his family so nobody else felt frogish and wanted to leap!

I like to do things a little differently, stealth has always been a way of movement. We landed in Cali a few hours later and kissed each other goodbye at the airport. I got into a towncar and was taken home.

Tomorrow is another day. When I arrived home I saw a package on my doorstep, "Hmm, that's funny. I wasn't expecting any packages today." Harper thought to herself as she got out of the car. She went over to the front door to see what the package was and it was addressed to Jackie Wellington, "that's mother's full name, who would be sending her mail to my house?" Harper takes the package into the house and sits it on the counter in the kitchen. The phone was ringing as she entered the door.

"Hi sis, yes I made it in." Harper says as she answers the phone. "How do you know it's me? Everytime through?" Skye says annoyed.

Cause I know you little sister, Shit, I practically raised you".

The two sister's chat a little while longer then Harper says goodbye to her baby sis and hangs up the phone. Harper gets ready to turn in for the night when she suddenly realizes she forgot about the package. She goes downstairs to the kitchen and turns on the lights. She grabs a knife to cut the tape that was holding it closed. As she opened the box there were documents and pictures and recordings of Mother from what looks like the FEDS handy work. Harper grows real concerned and begins looking over everything. They had so much evidence, bank accounts, storage spaces, phone call logs, property you name it , they had it.

"Fuck, what the fuck is this shit?"

"Mother never said a word to me about the FEDS or any kind of trouble she was having". Harper puts all the papers and things away in her safe and goes to bed. As she lay on her pillow she thought to herself, "We are gonna have to do something drastic, make a move out of this shit!"

The next morning Janelle wakes up to a ringing phone " Hello" she asks in a tired whisper.

" Hello, this is D, You up lil sis?" "I need to talk to you".

Janelle sits straight up in her bed and wakes right the hell up. "What's up D man?'

" Man, the FEDS is all over me and shit, they want me to snitch on Mother and y'all, but I didn't tell' em shit"!!

"Wait, wait back up, you were arrested? When?" she asks very calmly.

" Yeah" "Like a couple of weeks ago they approached me getting into my car coming out of the strip club one night right?"

"Yeah, and?" Janelle replied with an attitude by this point. " Well, they were just asking me, Do I still work for Jackie?,

Do I know they are close to taking her down?

Shit like that" "I didn't believe the shit cause, if you had all that, What the fuck ya'll jammin me up for, You know what I'm saying". " They trying to get some shit, that's what it is.

D, we just got back last night and you ain't never mentioned to any of us that you were arrested dude! What the fuck?

I know, but they had shit, so I felt like I handled it.

Alright, thanks for letting me know what's up and I'll call you later "Cool ma, see you soon".

Omg! What the fuck, is going on Janelle thought to herself. "I need to talk to my sisters."

So, J gets up, gets dressed, sends out a text to her sisters to meet up at a new restaurant just opened up downtown. Janelle jumps into her car and races downtown to meet her sisters, the news she had to relay to them was so fuckin deep, it had to be discussed in person. She arrives at the diner, as she starts to park she notices this car following her, so she busts a move around the corner real quick on they ass and shook they ass like dust.

Janelle drove back to the diner to talk with her sisters. Everyone got there around the same time, got out of their vehicles and grabbed a table in the back to have some privacy.

"So what's up Jill girl, why you got us out here at 3:00 in the fuckin morning crazy?" Skye asked her sister with an irritated voice.

"Look, y'all apparently Mother had some run-ins with the FEDS and never mentioned it to us. D called me tonight and told me that they asked him questions about Mother and his affiliation with her, about the businesses and shit.

"They know something if they sniffing this close," says Harper. "I got a package on my doorstep when we got back from our trip a couple of nights ago, and it was full of shit the FEDS had on Mother".

When was D arrested anyway? And, why didn't he tell me?

I asked the same question sis, He said he took care of it.

The sisters sat at the diner for a while longer talking about what the next move would be.Harper continued to tell them about what was in the box from the FEDS. photos, video, transcripts of telephone calls between Mother and Dante', us, everyone. over 800 pages of texts and phone calls. All kinds of incriminating shit on her businesses, real estate, etc.

I can't believe they had all this evidence and did nothing with it.

Mother had so many people on the payroll, I wouldn't be surprised if some fuckin FEDS made the list. It would make sense on a lot of shit, like how Mother was able to move like she did. The amount of respect on her name, was aspiring and fearful at the same time. Mother was a force!!

"So, what I'm going to do is go see Mother's attorney and see how much he knows and what he can tell me, I will call you guys when I leave his office" Harper tells her sisters.

"Bet, check y'all later" yelled Skye.

Skye left that meeting with all kinds of feelings and questions about her mother, things she always wondered, things she had heard. Never once asking anyone to clear up her assumptions, to tend to her silenced emotions, answer her unasked questions. Maybe one day she will get the nerve to ask her sisters to tell her who her Mother really was behind the Iron Fist!!

The next morning Harper got up early so she could get right down to business. She called the attorney to let him know that she will be stopping by soon. She goes downstairs to the kitchen and makes some coffee and English muffins. She walks back toward her bedroom passing by her 9 foot mirror in the hallway and looking at how all the stress from Mother's murder and all the deception around the camp, has her looking real thin.

I know I'm stressed out but, gosh damn Harp, you need to take better care of yourself girl! You know ain't nobody gonna do it for your ass.

Oh well onto the business at hand.

Harper continues on upstairs to shower and get dressed. She goes to the closest to choose one of her many power suits. Michael Kors,

Versace', no Armani, that's the one baby. As Harper slips herself in her fierce business attire and heads out the door to the attorney's office.

Upon arrival, Harper noticed she was being followed, some undercover asshole, anyway. Harper grabs her phone and takes a picture of his car and plates and continues on and enters the building. As soon as Harper walked in, the receptionist came right over to her and offered tea or coffee?

"No thank you, Is he busy?" Harper asked.

"No, he had a phone call but now you may go right in, he's been expecting you Ms. Wellington.

"Well Hello Harper , long time no see. How long has it been girl?". "I was so sorry to hear about your mother. So very tragic, she was a lovely woman".

"Thank you Mr. Carlson and the flowers you sent over to the Chapel were beautiful".

"The reason I'm here is I need to know everything you know about my mother's business. I would like to know what the FEDS know, I would like to know everything you know, I am at the top of the throne now, I need to know everything so my moves can go accordingly.

" I can totally understand where you're coming from, your mother had a very lucrative business. The FEDS came to her about a year ago asking all sorts of questions about her, her business, and who she deals with. Some of your mother's businesses are very legit, the nail shop on Fruitvale ave. in Oakland and the restaurant in Castro Valley."

"Well, that's great, we would like to liquidate and dissolve all of our mother's businesses, except the legit ones." "Can you start the paperwork for that and we'll take care of everything else." Harper explains to the attorney.

" No problem, I will get started on that right away," he replied. "Thank you Mr. Carlson, We will be in touch soon.

Now that Harper has talked to the attorney, things should move a little smoother or least give her time to set her plan in motion. She decides to take a ride down to the neighborhood to see how Dante' doing with the street business? When she hit the corner on the block, all you could see was that beautiful plum Mercedes with "BOSS" on the license plate. She spots Dante' down the block, she pulls over to park. As she gets out of the car, she can see someone talking to Dante', a man in a suit talking in front of the trap.

"What the fuck" she thinks to herself.

The man shakes Dante's hand as he walks him to his car. "Alright man, talk to you soon".

Harper walks up to Dante' and asks him. "Who the fuck was that?"

Dante responds with a shaky voice, " oh, he's just a dude that wants to get a large amount, but I don't know yet?

CHAPTER 7

As Harper and Dante' start talking, Harper asks to see the operation ledgers and information on its associates? D takes her in the house so he can show her exactly what's what.

" Where is the money?" Harper asks D. "It's put up sis, you need something?". What did you just say to me?

I apologize Harper, I meant no disrespect. If you say so!!

Anyway, I just got out of a meeting with my attorney and he let me know what the FEDS know about Mother's businesses. "The sisters and I feel we need to shut shit down for good and just go legit.

Legit, what does that mean?" Dante asks with fear in his heart, because he knew his time in the game was almost up.

" Yes, motherfucka. The FEDS are too close, and ain't nobody going to jail on my watch nigga!"

Harper phone rings, I'll take this in the office. It was Skye on the line, "Hey sis, what's happening?"

Nothing much, just sitting here at the trap talking to Dante' stupid ass and picking up all the money. I think we need to empty all the traps and pick up the money and take it to mother's house and count and decide, what's what?

I hear you Harp, this shit is getting way too wreckless out here in these streets, and you know I'm out here daily , so I know and the streets is talking to sis.

Call me when you leave the spot and we will meet up and Mother's? Cool, sis. See you then.

I knew there was some funny shit going on when some random ass dude comes through the door acting like he'd been there before, which I don't put past Dante's ass. D knows not to let no one in this mothafucka when I am here. What the hell is he thinking? I collected all the loot and walked into the living room and told Dante' to walk me to my car, I had my strap on me just in case a nigga get some courage.

Alright D , what was that?

My bad Harper, it will never happen again, I promise. Dude hella cool and he wanna do some business.

Where is he from? Northern Cali I think? You think?

What the fuck are you doing out here man, you need to get your shit together. Find out where this nigga from and all the shit! Call me when you get something, peace!

As I was pulling off this young man flagged me down, now usually I wouldn't stop for no random person but he seemed harmless. Plus, I got the steal so I'm good.

I rolled the window down and asked him how can I help you little man? He had to be all of 15 years old.

I want to spit my poem to you, I write poetry and I wanna see what you think? I respect you and how you carry yourself.

Well, ok let's see what you got? Ok here it go, When one thinks of the hood

The primary thought is guns and drugs When I think of the hood I think of laughs and hugs!

The word hood consists of history and culture Not dividing souls, snakes, and vultures.

They air bleeds with hard working souls Who pay there tolls who love their culture.

So they remain like moles. The grounds are dirty, why? That represents the struggle.

The knuckles are bleeding, why? That represents the hustle

The engines scream loud, why?

That represents the hustle.

Just know white, black, rich, or poor. We all should have each other!

Man, that was so beautifully written and spoken, you need to keep writing young man.

Here is a couple of dollars to let you know you can do anything and become successful!

A couple of dollars, there's 500 dollars here!!

Yes, enjoy it the right way buy yourself all the writing equipment you need to keep your dream alive, ok?

Yes ma'am.

Alright stay good. Bye!

I felt so warm inside, talking to and helping this kid. It made me miss my business with my kids I teach with Autism. I hope he does well. Now, back to business as usual. Let me call Skye to see where her fast ass is?

Girl, where are you?

On my way to mother's, I was just gonna wait for you there. Oh, ok well I will be there shortly!

Cool harp, cause girl I got some tea for you!! Well don't spill it until I get there crazy!

Ok.

I began to drive on the freeway bumping Mother's favorite song by Anita Baker You Bring me Joy.

Thinking of her and beginning to cry. I need to take care of this family now, I can hear her talking to me in my head. Harper you're my oldest daughter and I know I raised you to be the savage boss for the business and a strong woman for your sister's.

I know Mother, I hear you.

I arrive at the house and I see Skye's car there in the driveway. I walk up to the door and it flings open and i see my sister standing there with some nigga with a nine to her fucking head and another come up behind me real quiet like.

Put your fuckin hands up bitch!! I guess I'm late for the party!

Don't get smart bitch, you know why we here!!

I think you have the wrong address fellas but, i'm sure we can work out something.

Standing there with my hands in the air, I try to negotiate a compromise of some sort.

Ok, tell me what it is you want and i'll see if i can help you gentleman? Aww, come on, you mothafuckin hoes know what this is?

This is a fucking jack!!

For a minute i thought these were some niggas from Houston on some retaliation shit, but, no they were here to rob us.

Everybody knows mother is dead so every crackhead with an ounce of courage will be trying us. I expected this sooner or later, just not this soon.

What are you guys here for? Where's the safe bitch?

It's in the bedroom!

Skye says to the one that was holding the gun to her head at the door.

They both look so dirty and strung out it was pathetic. I looked at Skye to let her know I'm about to make a move, she looked as if she understood so I proceeded. I grabbed the wrist of the guy that was pointing his gun at me and rotated the gun right out of his damn hands. He never knew what hit his ass.

Now get yo ass up and face the fuckin wall How the hell yall get in here?

We heard that Ms. Jackie was gone. We thought no one would be here ma, we swear, we don't wanna hurt nobody really, we just wanted to get some money for some dope!

The two men were against the wall while me and Skye was trying to figure out what to do with them, these muthafuckas try to jump us!!

One of them takes Skye into one of the upstairs bedrooms, as she was going up the stairs you could hear her fighting for her life.

Fuck you nigga! What you gonna do bitch?

Kicking and screaming at him she manages to kick him in the nuts and he drops her tiny ass, she is all of 120 pounds wet, now, it's a fight.

The one downstairs with me had me on my back and choked me. I grab a vase on the table next to us and cracked his ass across his fucking head. He stopped choking me and grabbed his bleeding head. He charges at me and we go over the couch and out falls a nine millimeter Mother always kept something everywhere. We're both scrambling trying to reach the gun as it slides under the table. He was on top of me and hitting me in the face with what felt like every ounce of power he had. I managed to get an arm free during the struggle and hit him in the face with all my might!! I grabbed the gun and stood over him, bleeding from the mouth, nose and head, and shot him in the head and in the chest!!

Checkmate bitch! Do you know who you fucking with? Skye? Sister?

I muster up some energy to get upstairs to check on my sister. When I reach the top of the stairs I can hear Skye screaming and the man saying something. I think I was in and out of consciousness, because I couldn't hear what he was saying, just a lot of yelling. I walk into the bedroom and this asshole was on top of Skye trying to rape her. Her shirt was ripped off and her pants were almost there when I pointed the gun at him and shot his ass in the head and he fell off of her. She pushes him off of her and grabs the gun out of my hand and shoots him four more times in the face.

Fuck you muthafucka! You wanna fuck somebody you fuck? I can't believe this dirty crackhead was trying to rape me!

All of a sudden we heard a noise coming from downstairs, we creeped into the hallway at the top of the stairs so we could look down to see if we could see what the noise was? We began walking down the stairs when i say in my loudest voice

Who the hell is that? I will put a bullet in your ass!!

We look and it's our sister Janelle.

Oh my God, What happened?

Some niggas was in the house when i got here Skye starts telling Janelle and they were here to rob the house not expecting nobody to be here and I was here waiting for Harper to get here. They put guns to our heads and then we get control of the guns and then we get fucking attack. That shit happened so fuckin fast. Somehow we get separated and one takes me upstairs and tries to rape me!

Bitch! You know I'm heated than a muthafucka?

Girl, the one down here with Harper was choking her out so she fought him and ended up shooting his ass.

What? Where is the body?

In the living room near the fireplace Harper says to her sister crying. We need to get the fuck out of here and get to a hospital.

What about these damn bodies Harp?

Janelle, don;t worry I called Dante' and he's on his way here, he can come and clean this mess, don't trip!

Why is D on his way here anyway?

This shit is getting crazy sis, what are we gonna do? That won't be the last we see or hear from them and others like "them"!!

Harper, what do you think we should do?

I think the first thing we need to do is find Dante' and make sure he deals with this shit first then we need to come together and sell this big motherfucker and be done with at least this part.

Harper pulled her phone out of her Prada bag and called Dante' and told him what happened as much as she could over the phone.

Dante', I need you to get to mother's house now!! Fucking ASAP nigga. I'm down the street, what happened?

I need you to take care of something here at the house. No problem sis, I will be there in 2 minutes. One!

Dante' is on his way so we can get out of here Harper tells her sisters. I don't want anything like this to happen to us again Harp, Skye! You feel me, I could've lost you guys tonight, do you realize that?

I told you I want to dismantle this business, divide it up and let us get on with our lives.

I can't believe the asshole had a fuckin gun to my head!

Skye, you looked so scared when i showed up at the door, how long had they been here?

I don't know, maybe 20 minutes before you showed up. I told them I was alone hoping that they would just take some shit and leave but

I had my shit on me just in case. The nigga came out of nowhere and just grabbed my gun from behind my back.

How long were you here?

About an hour, I heard something in the kitchen break, like glass. So i came downstairs and there they were, fucking guns pointed right at me. It all happened pretty fast.

Who told them or sent these niggas here i wonder? What do you mean Harp?

I feel like our heads are on the chopping blocks, motherfuckers are gunnin for us sister, we need to keep our eyes open!

I understand sis, Harp I thought for a minute that they were here from.. I know don't say it, girl i was thinking the same thing.

What?

Houston bitch!

I know , let's get the fuck out of here! You got your shit on you J?

You know it!!

Good, call me when you get home you guys? We will!! They both answered at the same time.

We each pulled off in our exotic cars and all I could think about was it could've gone another way. Mother is still watching over us from above. Time to go home nurse these wounds and soak in my gigantic jacuzzi fucking tub!

Yesss!!

CHAPTER 8

When i got home Sincere was in the kitchen cooking dinner, What are you doing? It's like 11:30 at night sweetheart?

I know but I wanted to see you, I tried to call but no response and i looked at my key ring and noticed i haven't used my key in.... What the hell happened to you baby?

It's ok Sin, it looks a lot worse than it really is. Who did this to you/ and why?

I can't talk about this now, I'm going up to soak in the jacuzzi and nurse these wounds babe. You coming?

Do you need to go see a doctor or something, let me look at you?

No i don't but thank you for caring so much i tell him as i hold him around his waist.

So, you staying or what?

No, I think I'll let you do you tonight, enjoy the dinner! Sincere!!!

Shit, once again I send our relationship to another level, he;ll be alright. I ain't never chased after a nigga and i'm not about to start.

I can't tell him anything about what's going on because I don't know yet if he's the one. I layed in my tub thinking of everything that's been going down lately and I came up with a theory!

Dante" is so fuckin distant lately it's making me suspicious of him. I wonder if this nigga is talking to the FEDS to try and get himself a deal, can't put nothing past a nigga. I reach for my phone and call my sisters what they think, but before I do that let me pour myself a shot of hennessy.

Girls, what's up? Everyone ok?

Yes sister, says Skye.

What's on your mind? asks Janelle.

Well sisters, I think there is a rat among us! What bitch? What you mean by a rat?

Skye, not y'all stupid, Dante' has been hella distant lately. He ain't been calling and checking in and shit, oh and when i went to the trap, he was talking to a man in a suit and an all black limo. What the fuck is going on?

Did you ask him what's up with the suit? Hell yes, Skye, I asked him. Well?

He said it was some work, but it just ain't been sitting right with me though. I want to put someone on him

Skye, you got somebody that could be invisible but get us some intel? Hell yeah, he likes one of my dancers hella much, i got this sis!!

Cool, get on that pronto. You know how it is when I feel something in my gut babygirl.

I know Harp, got you!!

Now that Skye has Dante' as a target I can finally figure out what to do about the business we inherited from our loving Mother. I don't want to make my sisters feel any type of way but, I need to do something that will make sure that all of us are taken care of. I wonder if the streets are talking anything about the murders at Mother's house a few months ago?

I will call the cleaner today, she'll take care of that shit real quick and quiet! Ok, time to get some much needed sleep mama, got a lot of shit to do, need to be on point for the plan to work. So I'll send out some bait and see what I catch!!

The next day came and I was awakened by a doorbell ring.

Who the hell is that? I say to myself.

I go toward the kitchen and look at the security cameras, it's Sincere what The hell does he want now, I don't have time to deal with him right now.

Hi honey, I say to him as he opens the front door. What are you doing here sweetie?

I need to talk to you Harper. What the hell is going on? I always thought maybe you were into something other than the businesses you own. I just never put 2 and 2 together.

I am so busy with the business stuff and all, is there something particular you want to talk about now? Other than my Mother's business?

Yes, I want more time with you baby. When are we gonna have time to take this relationship to the next level?

Babe, I get it!

But, you need to understand that there is a lot of bullshit with trying to get Mother's estate in order, trying to be there for my sisters, and trying to decide what's next. I expect you to be there for me and be patient with all that I'm going through, Sin. I love you terribly but, give me some time sweetheart, ok?

Fine Harp, do you and as your man I will be there for you and whatever you need, im here!!

Sincere hugs Harper so tight it was almost like he wasn't gonna see her again or something.

By the way, I heard some shit in the street about you and your sister's having some trouble with some niggas. Look Harper, I know you can take care of yourself but a nigga ain't about to sit on the sidelines and watch shit just go down around me.

I understand Sin, I will let you know everything you need to know soon. I'm just trying to keep you as safe as possible.

Cool, talk to you tomorrow Harp! Later babe!

As Sincere is leaving, Harper begins to think about how much she would love to be with Sin on an everyday basis, but life is happening and I gotta take care of the family first!!

What the fuck is the streets exactly talking about us? I need to call the sisters to see what's what, but better yet let me call Dante' punk ass and find out why he ain't been hitting me up. Let me call Skye and see if she got anything to report on this wack ass nigga.

Yo, Skye what up?

Shit, what are you doing sis?

Nothing girl, just had to do the fuckin Young and the Restless with Sincere ass. What's his problem?

He wants shit to move faster than they can right now, and he wants to know what we are doing about what the streets are saying about Mother's estate. He said some niggas was talking shit about what might of happened to our Mother or something.

Girl, you need to find out what he knows and who he has been talking to.

You know we can't trust nobody right now, mothafuckas is trying to take us the fuck out! Let me do some investigating on Sincere? Sure, let me know what you find out!!

Anyway, what if anything did you find out about Dante' sneaky ass?

Oh, it's getting handled, I'm close to some juicy ass tea and I'm waiting on some evidence as well.

Ok, when you find out anything let me know sister! For sure, love!! One!!

Oh my god Skye, what are you doing lying to your sister? I need more evidence before we do anything and before I can tell them anything. Matter of fact let me continue that mission now.

Harper is at home in the office doing some paperwork when the phone rang, Hello!

Hi, is this Harper Wellington? Who is this?

I'm sorry ma'am, my name is Justin Vangould and I got your number from your employee and I need to speak with you about a very sensitive matter. Can we meet?

Where did you get my number?

I went to your school in Atlanta and your assistant gave me the necessary numbers in order to reach you.

Ok, you've reached me, how can I help you Mr. Vangould?

The contents of this information is extremely sensitive ma'am, and we should speak in person.

ok , where would you like to meet?

This is your city, where do you suggest?

How about you leave me your number and i will call you with a time and venue. No worries, have a great day Ms. Wellington, talk to you soon.

You too, goodbye.

What the fuck was that? I need to call my sisters and I also need to call Tito so he can do some recon work on this Mr. Vangould!!

I really miss Mother, I have been thinking a lot about her lately. Waking up this morning I was thinking about my sisters and how they must be feeling about Mother being gone. We haven't spoken about her that much, but I know they miss her too. I think we need to visit Mother's grave and mourn properly. I'll give the girls a call and set it up. I wonder if Tito found out anything about our mystery man? And, where the hell is Dante'? Something is going on and I ain't feeling none of this shit. I've been sitting thinking lately about everything that has transpired since mother died and shit is weird. FEDS lurking around, Dante' ass disappearing for weeks, niggas breaking into the house, what the fuck? We need to get to the bottom of this, and soon!! Let me call Skye to see if she heard anything. Harper's phone begins to ring..

Hello?

What up nigga?

You so stupid girl, what up with you Skye?

You heard anything about Dante'? You know that nigga been missing for a few weeks now.

Yeah, that's why I'm calling sis, they found Dante' in a car in Vegas with his throat slashed in the fucking desert bitch.

What??

Yeah sis, the fuckin Vegas PD called me because i was the last number on his call log, i had a miss call from him but i was busy with work and shit, now I don't know what the fuck.

What did the police say, do they know anything yet? Not from what I can see.

Call Janelle let her know what up, I'm gonna hit the streets, shake some leaves see what fall the fuck out. Somebody knows something. My nigga would not have been in vegas alone.

Alright Harper, I'll talk to you later, call me if you need me. Cool, be careful. One!!

CHAPTER 9

Harper and her sister's have a big problem on their hands. There is a rat in the family and they need to figure out what the FEDS have on them and their Mother's business.

Damn, man. I have to find out what's going on with my sister Janelle? I haven't talked to her in a few weeks and I think Skye said she hasn't talked to her. What is going on with this family? It seems like Dante' has met his untimely demise and now I know that the FEDS is really fuckin circling. What I'm gonna do is get the sisters together and do some recon of our own!!

Let me call the trap and see what these niggas is doing with my fuckin money! Where is these dumb ass fools? (phone ringing).

Hello?

What up my nigga? What is it looking like over there?

Ah sis it's gravy all day, I heard what happened to my nigga man, so what's happening with that whole situation sis?

I don't know anything right now, we're gonna fly down in a few days to see if we can find out the truth, you know?

Yeah man, we gotta find out what the fuck went down.

So the reason for my call is to see if y'all have been having any trouble or anything happen lately out of the ordinary?

Naw, I ain't seen shit, I'll ask around though.

Well I'm on my way to you soon so we can talk further. Ok, cool ma. See you soon.

One!

Now all I need to do is get dressed and get this fuckin day started. Go to the closet and grab me Gucci pumps and a badass Gucci jumpsuit that gives my ass a look that won't quit, ok boo! Shit,

Harper is a fashionista, she just doesn't act like it. Her appearance is and has always been a part of her personality. She admires her selection for the day in the mirror and heads for the door.

Ok, looking expensive, time to make some moves out here.

As Harper walks out of her house to her car she sees a handsome man approaching her. By the cut of his suit, you can tell he was a FED. to bad too cause this motherfucka is fine ass hell.

How can I help you sir?

Hello, are you Ms Harper Wellington? Yes, what is this about?

Well Ms. Wellington, I am investigating the murder of an acquaintance of yours. Really, who would that be?

A man by the name of Dante' Sacks. He was killed in his car in the city of Las Vegas.

Yes, I have heard about that, we went to school together in junior high school. I don't understand how I can help you with that though agent.

I believe you can Ms. Wellington, We looked through Mr. Sacks phone and found a few numbers and we came across yours.

Ok, I saw Dante' at a club in Miami last year and we exchanged numbers, no crime.

All though that may be true Ms. Wellington, we found out through our investigation that Mr. Sacks contacted you a few months ago.

And?

Well, would you mind telling me the nature of that call?

Yes, I do. I have nothing to do with whatever Dante' may have been involved with or know who in the world has reason to hurt him. If you have any other questions for me , please direct them to my attorney. Here is his card and it was very nice chatting with you agent but I must get to my errands.

No problem Ms. Wellington, I will do that. You take care now, let me get your door for you.

Thank you, you're very handsome for a FED.

I appreciate that Ms. Diamond, you're very beautiful yourself. I thank you as well. Have a nice day agent.

Nice car, 2016 Audi huh?

Oh yeah, nothing but the best baby.

He begins to follow Harper down the driveway and out the gate, she makes a right and he turns left.

Wow, that was intense!! What the hell are they fishing for, I know his FED nose thinks he smells something. I better put a tail on him so I can see what they might know.

Let me go over to Janelle's house to check on her to see if either her or Skye got interrogated?

Harper gets onto the freeway on the way to her sister's house, when she sees Skye over at the gas station getting into it with someone.

Oh shit, let me see what this shit is!

Harper pulls off the freeway ramp and pulls into the gas station to see her sister Skye with some girls head in a head lock move.

What the fuck sister?

Harper gets in between them to stop the fight and find out what it's about.

Harp, this bitch sees me pull up to the pump and then when I get out, she walks up to me and starts asking me all kinds of questions about Dante'!

What??? Why is she asking you that shit?

I don't know, all I know is this bitch got me fucked up!

Look girl I don't know who you are but , you should know who we are!

Oh, I know exactly who you are, y'all the same bitches that let something happen to my brother!

What, Dante, is your brother? What is your name? Because clearly you don't know us very well or the reputation, because there is a certain level of respect I will demand from you. It's been well earned. Now, come correct and we might be able to help you

Carmen is my name, and I apologize for the disrespect ma!. All I know is they found him in Vegas shot dead in his car.

Well, you know just as much as we know. As a matter of fact, give us your number and if we find out anything we'll call you ok?

Cool

Alright, you go that way and I will take my sister this way. Sis what the fuck?

Naw, this bitch hella out of pocket right now, bitch don't ask me shit, I don't fuck wit Dante' like that you know?

Yeah, anyway forget her, what were you doing over here this early? Even though it's 12 noon, that's early for you.

I was coming to see if you got a visit from some fine ass FED this morning asking about what happened to Dante', how do I know him and shit. I'm like what nigga? Here is the number for my attorney, bye Felicia!!

Ha, ha you hella stupid girl! Where are you off to Harp?

Going to Janelle's house to let her know what's been going on, I haven't talked to her in a few weeks, so I was going to go over and check on her. Have you talked to her?

No, not in a few weeks either, we kinda had a little argument and I hung up on her. It was real fuckin stupid now that I think about it.

What was the fight about?

Sister shit, stupid girl not even worth mentioning. Do you wanna ride with me over there?

Yeah, let's do it.

Alright cool.

Harper and Skye head over to Janelle's mansion in Blackhawk and when they show up, they are stunned. Her door is wide open and her car is gone.

What the fuck is this shit? Asks Skye.

I don't know, but let's check it out. You got that thang on you? Always!

Cool, lets go, you go around back, I'll go in through the front, holla if you see or hear anything ok?

Yeah I got it!

Harper enters the house from the front open door calling for her sister. Janelle?Janelle? Are you here honey?

Harper looks all through the living room and begins to head upstairs, calling her sister's name. Gun out in front of her as she enters her sister's bedroom, she is frozen by what she sees, her sister is laying on the floor of her bathroom shot to death with her gun in her hand. Harper closes the door as she hears Skye coming up the stairs.

Go downstairs and call 911 now!! Why, what's up? Nelle, sister you ok? Call 911 Skye right fuckin now!!!

Harper held her head on the door as she cried for her sister, she leaned down to cover her sister's head which had a perfect round hole in it.

Blood was everywhere, Sis put up a good ass fight it looks like though.

Skye honey? Are the police on their way? Harper yells through the bathroom door, she doesn't want Skye to see her like this.

Yes , I just called them. Skye tries to open the door, turning the knob as hard as she could. Why is the door locked?

Go downstairs and wait for the police Skye, now! No!! She is my sister too!

Now let me see her damn it!! alright.

No!,No!,No! Why man? Harp, who would do this? First D now our sister, shit is getting so fuckin dangerous.

It's ok baby sis, don't you worry! We goin deal with this shit! Trust and believe me!

Dangerous is what this family does baby, we got this!! I put that on Mother!!

The sisters give each other a comforting but vengeful look Then, the howling of the sirens was getting louder they could hear the police outside.

We need to find out who did Dante' in Vegas to see if there is a connection to this shit.

Looks like she got off at least 4 shots at the muthafucka though. You think we need to get her gat?

Naw, let the police find it in her hands, that way they know she tried to defend herself. Her shit registered!

Here, put our shit in the safe until the police leave, we don't need the extra aggravation right now.

Yeah, plus I saw some blood drops outside in the back near the fence.

Good, maybe the fuckin police will be able to find who did this. They better find them before we find them!

Where the fuck is her car?

Good evening ladies, I'm sorry we are meeting under these terrible circumstances, and I am so sorry for your loss.

My name is Detective Ryan Logan, I will be the detective on your sister's case. Which one of you is Harper?

I am, how can I help Detective Logan?

You are your sister Janelle Wellington's emergency contact, I just want to get all the information I can so we can solve this awful crime.

Well, we want to know what the hell happened here at my sister's gated home? That's good, maybe we can help each other?

Do you know anyone that would want to hurt your sister?

No! Hell No! My sister helped people; she didn't have any enemies. Harper says annoyed by the question.

Looking at this young, black man, with judgment in his eyes. Wondering how can this young woman afford this exquisite property? He seems to be more focused on us than my beautiful sister.

I apologize ladies, we will keep you informed as the case develops.

Here is my card, my cell phone is on the back, call me if you guys hear anything. Yes sir, Detective.

Oh, one more thing, Are you the Wellington sister'? As in Jackie Wellington?

Yes, she was our Mother, and what the hell does that have to do with the fact that my sister was just murdered in her own fuckin home!

Just wanting to get all the information.

Oh, don't you worry we will get to the bottom of this asap Ms.Harper. He says as he stares at us.

Is there anything else Detective?

Yes, Ms. Harper, where were you today between the hours of 3:00 pm and 5:30pm?

I was at work doing some inventory. Why? Just routine questions ma'am.

What about you Ms.Skye? I just got into town today,

Oh yeah? Where were you returning from and at what time was that?

I just got back from Miami, my flight got in around 12:30 pm and I was tending to my business there.

Ok, ok, just trying to get all the information ma'am. Yeah, so you've said.

The Detective smiles and says

You girls get home safe, and call me if you need anything. Thank you, goodbye.

The sister's began to walk toward Harper's car and go home when Skye's phone started ringing.

Who dis?

Is this Skye Wellington? Who the hell is this?

Listen, and listen well. If you want to know who did your sister tonight, you will meet me at San Antonio park over on foothill ave. at 11:00pm tonight?

What, how did you get my number?

I'm trying to help you guys, just be there and bring Harper too. Click! Who was that? Harper asks Skye

Some man who sounded hella scared and has information on what happened to Janelle.

What? Where does he wanna meet Skye?

San Antonio park in Oakland at 11:00 tonight girl.

I don't know Harp, this shit sounds shady as fuck though!

I tell you what, we go call up the squad and have them handle that. Me and you are going to Mother's house, I always felt safe there.

Let's go baby sis, we all we got now!

Harper and Skye ride all the way to their Mother's house in total silence.

Each of them tore up inside about what just happened. It's almost like reality was just sitting in, their sister is dead! Harper looks over at Skye, as she sees one full tear drop fall from her baby sister's face realizing in that moment that they must protect each other at all times from now on.

They pull up to their mother's gate and go into the house. Come here baby sis.

Yes big sis?

Harper puts her arms around her babysitter and holds her. We are hurting so bad and looking at her and feeling her heart beat so fast. I know it's beating with vengeance as the fuel.

You ok sweetheart?

No, we just lost Mother only under a year, and now we gotta do that shit all over again. And for what?

Skye, this is what we're going to do.

CHAPTER 10

Harper and Skye are in the living room, looking at one another waiting for the other one to move first. They both knew what the other was thinking, Revenge!! Skye layed down on the leather couch and began to just sob and cry so hard, I had to go over and literally hold her in my arms to console her. I can't believe this is happening to us. First, my Mother gets murdered and we still got digging there to do, now, my beloved sister who doesn't fuck with nobody gets bodied by some coward ass, pussy ass niggas!

The sister's sit together and drink tea while talking about the good times with their Mother and sister. Harper walks into the office after Skye finally falls asleep on the couch. As she walks into the office, you can feel Mother's presence in there. She walks over to the big desk where her Mother used to sit to make money moves!! While sitting at her Mother;s beautiful mahogany desk, she begins to make funeral arrangements, she turns from the desk to ask Skye for her input on the funeral, but forgets she was asleep.

Harper sat at the desk continuing with the arrangements when she got a call from that Detective from my sister Janelle's house.

Hello?

Hi, this Detective Ryan, do you remember me? Of course Detective , how can I help you?

Oh well, I told you I would keep you posted on all information regarding your sister's murder.

Right?

Well, we picked up two suspects a couple of hours ago driving on Hwy 1. Really, how did you guys find them?

They were being pulled over for a broken tail light and when the officer saw the suspects in the car and then he ran the plates, it came back as a car in Janelle Wellington's name.

What? My sister's car was in her driveway.

Yes, yes you are correct but apparently, she had another. I'm starting to think maybe your sister knew her attackers. Anyway, I just wanted to give you a heads up on the progress.

Well, thank you so much Detective Ryan, I really appreciate that you have a great day.

Oh Ms. Diamond one more thing, did you know that your sister had an office space in Castro Valley which is where the car they were found in was registered to.

No I did not. But I'm sure my sister had all her licenses in order. Yeah you're probably right. Talk to you soon Ms. Wellington.

Goodbye Detective.

What the hell did he want? Skye asks with an attitude.

He was giving us an update on the case, they found two guys on Hwy 1 trying to get out of town and the interesting thing is they were driving one of Jill's cars. Crazy right?

Hell yes.

Anyway I'm gonna go get dressed and go get this funeral business out of the way. I need to get that started, plus I want to go by her place of business and make sure everything is ok. Or to close shit down, whatever's needed!

Ok, well I'll be upstairs so call me if you need any help with the details sis. I will, you go get some rest, I got this!

Ok, I can't believe she's gone man!!

Harper looked at her sister as she walked up the stairs so slow and crying in her kleenex. This has to be the hardest shit to be going through again this year. Our mother's funeral was just under a year ago and here we go burying our sister, niggas think that there is a breach in the family and maybe it has but I'll tell you one thing, I will be getting to the bottom of this shit real quick!!

I think we will use the same place as we did for mother, they were very kind and helpful to us. As Harper was deciding what colors and clothes to put on her little sister it began to hit her, she put her hands over her eyes and began to cry. Harper is so used to being the one to just jump up and take care of everything and everybody. Harper loves her sisters so much. She got on her knees and began to pray.

How am I going to do this again Lord, please help me. I ask you father God to put your hands around us and keep us oh Lord, we are so hurt and confused right now father God and I ask you to take the pain away Lord, help my sister Skye deal with this loss Lord, she is the baby and I can't lose her too, I'll never make it!! In Jesus name I pray. Amen!

Harper stood up and wiped her eyes and began to plan and strategize. Niggas gonna feel the wrath of the Diamond sisters just like in the old days when Mother was in these streets laying niggas down!! Time to rehash some fuckin history!!

Harper goes upstairs to tell Skye she was going by Janelle's business and checks everything out, but when I got up there she was already in the bathroom and in the shower.

Hey sis?

What up?

I was about to go by Jill's business and check up on thangs you know? Well damn hold up a minute, I wanna roll! Skye told Harper.

Ok girl, let's get it going boo.

Harper and Skye get dressed and jump in the Bentley. So you end up getting a lot of details together Harp?

Yes, I pretty much got everything done. I just decided that we would just have it at the same place we did for mother.

What do you think about that? Are you ok with that or did you want something different? I mean your input is just as important honey.

I know Harper, I agree. We are going to do it real big for sis, she deserved it, you know?

You're right!

Driving down the driveway to leave their mother's home Skye spots some niggas sitting in a car on the corner, a black SUV Cadillac.

What the fuck is this sis?

I don't know lil sis, but I'll tell you what. You got that thang? Always! I told you that before.

Alright, we're gonna pass them slow enough to catch a look at anybody.

Harper starts to drive slowly down to the stop sign at the corner, she take a look to her left and notices that there were four niggas in the car. Harper looked at the one in the back and recognized him.

Skye, I think I know the one in the back. For real, from where though?

He was trying to holla at a bitch at a gas station not too long ago, what the hell would he be doing here?

Call the goons, send them to mother's house, your condo, and my house right now!!!

I'm on it sis! Skye looks at her sister and can tell she is fed up with all this shit.

The sisters head down to their mother's house to check shit out, and when they pulled up onto the street, it was extremely dark and the street lights were out over mother's house. Harper can see the car she put in front of the house with the goons inside as she drives slowly down the street. Harper then parks the car and turns to her sister and tells her what's about to go down.

Ok Skye, shit is about to get real!! We have been here before, watch your ass. I'm gonna go and check the goons, you go around back and use the secret tunnel that you access from the street!

Ok sis I got you. Hit me if you got any issues. I will, go!!

Harper slowly walks towards the car with her goons inside and when Harper taps on the window, as she is scooched down next to the car there was no response. Harper then proceeds to look inside the car and there they were, dead!! Two shots to the head!

Fuck!!! What the hell is going on??

Harper starts to think and remembers a friend having some info on those niggas at mother's funeral in the red suits. So, Harper calls Pat Combs. She was mother's closest friend and knew everything about her. Harper goes to the secret entrance to enter the house and to catch up with Skye.

Skye, where are you?

Harper enters through the bookcase in the study, and she doesn't hear anything back from her sister as she calls for her. Harper slowly walks through the study into the main living room looking around making sure whoever killed her folks are not still in the house.

Harper heads towards the kitchen, gat out, ready for whatever! She finds the maid dead on the floor next to the kitchen, sick, she checks her neck for a pulse and is shocked that the body is still warm! They're still here!!

Skye? Skye?

Harper heads upstairs to the bedrooms and clears the master bedroom then she walks down the hallway pointing that thang in front, vest on tight. All of a sudden Skye comes out of the hallway bathroom yelling,

Sister , it's me!!

Oh shit sis, girl I called for you, why didn't you answer me? Well I was tied up with the nigga I found in the office.

What happened?

I was creeping through the house checking for anyone and when I got upstairs to the office, there he was trying to get into the safe.

Did you take care of that? You know I did!

I walked up behind that nigga and slit his fuckin throat! Just like mother taught us!!

Shit, where is he?

Laying in there dead as fuck on the floor. What about the rest of the house? Clear?

Yes everything seems to be here, nothing else was touched.

I wonder who these fools are? And what the fuck do they want? Skye, I need you to call the cleaner, now!!

Let me check this safe to see what the hell they were looking for?

Harper goes over to the safe and opens it, to the sisters surprise, there were three ledgers sitting in there and about 250.000 in cash. Harper and Skye begin to read the ledgers and turn to look at each other, and at the same time say Damn!!!

Sister, mother has dirt on cops, judges, and even counsel men.

Skye , do you know what we got here? Bitch, this is why we all got a damn target on our backs. They probably think we already knew all of this. Here's what we are about to do...

Harper calls Pat Combs to see what info she could give.

Hello Pat, hi baby, how are you honey? I was meaning to give you girls a call after the funeral but you know I got busy and..

It's ok, the reason I'm calling is, me and Skye need to come see you and ask you some questions about my mother and what's been going on. I don't wanna talk over the phone though.

Ok baby, you guys can come over tomorrow, I'll be here. Ok Ms. Pat, see you soon.

Ok bye!!

So sis we going to go to her house tomorrow and see what's up on that end. I'm thinking that these ain't regular niggas trying to cap us, it's fuckin cops!!

What?? Do you really think so?

Yes, because we can't seem to find who is behind this, and we would've found out by now. Let's go to the cabin in Tahoe and go over these Ledgers with a fine tooth comb, so we can see what's our next move.

Cool, let go!!

We head up Hwy 50 toward the Sierra's to get to the cabin. As we ride Skye begins to cry, I look over at my baby sister with sadness in her eyes and revenge in her heart! I didn't say anything to her, I just put my hand on top of her hand and gave her that moment of grieving she was so obviously in. I had nothing on my brain but vengeance and malice. Looking at all the white snow and mountains all around her, the phone rang.

Hello?

Hello, hey is this Harper?

Yes, who dis?

Oh, you don't know me but, I was a close friend of your mother's. Really, how did you get my number?

That's not important right now, I have some very sensitive information to give you and your sister. By the way, I heard about what happened to your sister Jill. I am so sorry, you have my deepest sympathy.

Thank you, where would you like to meet and when, what did you say your name was?

Paul, Paul Combs.

Well, I'm kinda out of town right now, leave me your number so I can call you when I get back to the Bay Area.

Sure, 510-333-1445

Ok, cool. I will hit you up soon. Hey, what made you reach out to me now?

Your mother gave me specific instructions, that if anything happened to her, to give you an envelope she left for you.

Well, you're a little late sweetheart. My mother was killed almost a year ago.

I know, I was out of the country when your mother was tragically murdered. But, when I heard about your sister Jill and what happened, I knew I didn't have much time. I needed to contact you right away.

Ok, we definitely need to meet up asap!! What about tomorrow? That works for me, any place in particular in mind?

Yes, call me in the morning and we will go from there. I think we've said enough on the phone.

I will. Goodnight Harper. Goodnight.

Harp, who was that?

Girl, that was a man claiming to be a very close friend of Mother's. He says he needs to meet up with us asap, he has an envelope that mother left for us in case anything happened to her.

Well damn, he's a little late.

That's what I told him, but he said he was out of the country when mother died.

Convenient!!

Slow down sis, I'm already on it, we need to check this nigga out first. I'm gonna call Roscoe when we get to the cabin. I need him to find out what Mr. Combs' intentions are.

Very good idea. How far are we from the cabin? We'll be there in about 20 minutes. stop?

Cool, I gotta piss hella bad bitch!!

You so crazy Skye, there's a gas station at the next exit, you want me to.

Hell naw, I wanna use our own toilet shit, they're heated!!

The sister's laugh together and drive on up to the cabin. The whole way there I couldn't think of anything but what could possibly be in those ledgers and does Mr. Combs know anything about them? Whatever is going on, mother must have gotten info on someone very important. All they have is each other now.

Harper and Skye are realizing that they are deeper than they thought.

The cabin was a good idea for Harper.

Yeah, I knew we needed a place away that no one knows we have and strategize this shit out sis, you know?

Fo sho big sis! I got you.

Finally, they arrive at the cabin. When they pull up the driveway, its pitch fuckin black everywhere. The property is deserted but the security lights don't come on automatically. The girls sit in the car for a minute to scan the property before they make a move.

You see anything Skye? No, you?

No, what the fuck is going on with the lights?

I don't know. No one knows about this place so maybe it's just a coincidence Harp. let's go.

We get out of the car and head up to the front door, when all of a sudden, Shots rang out.

The sister's pulled out their shit and began to shoot back at the muthafuckas.

Do you see anybody Skye?

No Harp, what the fuck is happening? Fuck this shit, get the door open Harper!!

It is, get the fuck in here.

Shut the door bitch, they still fucking shooting!!

I got it!, stay low and keep the lights off for now. Let's go upstairs to the attic, I got a panic room installed last year in case Mother ever had trouble.

Ok run Skye!!

The moment they got into the panic room, Harper cut on all the security equipment and looked for the shooters.

Damn Harp, you wasn't bullshittin when you got this shit.

Hell naw, you never know what the fuck can go down in this crazy ass business we're in.

Do you see them anywhere?

Not yet Skye, but I will. The cameras are all equipped with night vision, I will be spotting their ass in a minute though. You look at those three screens and I will check these three screens, ok?

Yea, got you.

Ok I got yo ass now, they're in the backyard near the lake. I can see them coming toward the house from the dock, opening that steel crate over there Skye.

This one?

Yeah, that one. Get your weapon of choice and throw me something out too.

What's your plan?

I say we can corner them when they enter the kitchen from the back door, that's their only point of entry right now. Here put these on!

That's what's up sis, night vision goggles, yeah!! So , let's head downstairs on my count ok?

Alright!

One, two, three, Go! Move, move!!

As we crept downstairs in the pitch black darkness, we had the advantage. From what I could see there were only five I counted. Ok, they're in the kitchen, you go left Skye I'm gonna go this way. Shoot at everything, you got me??

Yes, I got you!!

Go!

As Harper is walking through the hallway to the kitchen she sees three of them, here is her opportunity to kill them all at one time. Harper began to shoot, she killed all three men, she stood there looking at them as they lay on the floor, dead and bleeding everywhere. Time felt like it stood still for a second.

I know they heard them shots, I need to find Skye.

Harper starts walking toward the living room and she sees another one bending over the table trying to read something. Harper slowly walks up behind the man and shoots directly in the back of the head.

One left she thought to herself, where the hell is Skye, at that moment she heard shots coming from the front living room, as she follows the noise she sees Skye shooting the last asshole in the chest four times and then the execution shot, right to the fuckin head. Harper calls out for her sister and Skye turns and looks at her sister as she stands over the man she just blew away and says, yes??

Are you ok?

Yes sis I'm good, let's see who these niggas is! I agree with that shit, who are these fools??

So, the sister's look at all the faces under the masks, to their surprise two of them they knew.

As Harper and Skye start to remove the masks off the shooters, Skye notices a tattoo on one the niggas left forearm. Skye begins to yell out,

I know this nigga! This muthafucka was at my club last month causing a lot of noise and started a fight in my shit, I had to put his punk ass out.

How do you know it's him Skye?

Because sis, when the fight at the club broke out, my bouncers went over to take control of the situation and this nigga popped off and broke the hand of one of my bouncers. So, I came out of my office to see what's the commotion and this muthafucka right here was doing all the talking.

Oh who is this bitch supposed to be?

I walked my fine ass down the stairs and told him..

This is my establishment you are misbehaving in, so I'm gonna need you and your immature ass friends to come back when you grow up boo boo!!

Girl, you can tell his ego was bruised, so, typical nigga he started saying what he can do and shit, anyway my goons ushered that ass out of the club and on the way out he pointed at me talking about Bitch, I'll see you again!!

Let's bring them all in the house, so we can see what's what. Right sis.

The sisters go round up all the shooters and brought them into the kitchen.

There in their mother's kitchen, on the floor lay five shooters who were sent to take their ass out. They need to get down to the bottom of it. Harper started searching their pockets and devices. Skye began taking all the masks off and took pictures of them for identity later.

These niggas were for hire sis.

Of course they were Skye, someone out there thinks we know something or have something very fuckin important. Let's put these fools downstairs in the cellar, throw them down the covered well. No one will ever find their ass!!

Alright, let's get rid of these fools, they are giving me the creeps anyway.

Yeah right, bitch! We been capping niggas since we was eighteen, mother knew what she was doing.

Ok! Skye says laughing.

As the sisters come back upstairs they're both thinking long and hard about every motherfucka that ever crossed them. It seems like someone out there is pulling the strings in this crazy ass puppet show. Harper grabs the fire poker as she stokes the fire as it was going out, looking into the flames made her reminisce about when they were growing up. Mother raised us on her own accord. She did things her way. When each of us turned a certain age she made us participate in a sort of ritual with us. At sixteen she takes you out to eat, just you and her. She starts to tell you what her Mother does for a living and how we can live so lavishly. Then after lunch and the talk, she takes you up to the hills and that's where you shoot your first animal. Usually a deer or a wild dog. After you killed it she would say, Now, that's how you take down a dog.

Then you two would go back to the car, have a great conversation and that would be that we would go on with life as usual. When each of us turned twenty one she would take you on a drive to one of the trap houses and once we get there, mother would walk in and everyone stood at attention, trying not to get on her bad side or fuck up at all. Then she'd talk to the nigga she left in charge and ask what's what? Once he run down the who was fucking up and who was making money, she would make an example out of the muthafucka fucking up.

She would tell them to come to the backyard and kneel before her daughter, then she would tell him what he did wrong,

Never listen to explanations, they're excuses baby!! Now do what mother taught you.

She handed me the gloc and I pointed it at his head and pulled the trigger and ended him execution style. Mother says that's the best way to make sure they're dead. Everyone would be freaked out of their mind looking at this woman giving her daughter such a responsibility. But, everybody always heard of it but when they had the opportunity to see it in person, it makes you even more scared of her. Mother made sure to tell us everything she did had a rhyme and a reason. Mother was a very strong and take no shit type of woman, she made sure muthafuckas would be afraid of her in life and in death. I guess someone didn't get the memo.

Shit, apparently not. I don't know what the hell is going on but this phone I got off one of them fools laid the fuck out in the kitchen should tell us something.

Oh, it seems like we have a few acquaintances in common, Skye, check this out.

Holy shit Harp, is that who I think it is?

Fuck yeah, and now the games began lil sister. I need you to go upstairs to the panic room to gather us a couple of bags together. We're gonna need lots of fire power, night vision goggles, the black suits, shit bitch, you know what to pack. It's time to find out who's pulling who's strings, you know.

Yeah, I got this sister. What are you going to do?

First things first, call the cleaner then call Mr. Combs to see what exactly is in that envelope he was so adamant about us seeing.

It's got to be something pertaining to all this mayhem we're going through. Because if you think about it, we don't really have any enemies. We inherited all these from Mother. I can handle the regular haters, but these are trained muthafuckas, hit men, niggas for hire to kill us. Makes you wonder why? Since they going so hard.

Ok, I'll go upstairs to get everything together.

Ok, be careful. Keep your eyes open, this damn mansion has a lot of places for niggas to hide. Fuckin roaches!!

Harper sits in the office looking into the phone of the men she just killed.

All of a sudden, as she scrolls through the pics and video she sees someone they know very well..

Ain't this about a bitch, I never trusted this nigga. Always at Mother's feet like an eager and obedient dog. As Harper looks at some video she notices the face of a traiter, Dante' punk ass. There was a video of him at a meeting with these men sent to kill us, taped what looks like six months or so ago a table meeting where Dante' snake ass is giving them instructions on what he believes to be a way to catch us slipping or with our guards down. Dante' should've known me better than that! His bad!! There were also a few numbers that needed to be checked out by Roscoe. Let me call Ms. Pat back so I can see what she knows.

Hello?

Hey Ms. Pat ma'am, how are you today? I'm good, is that you Harper?

Yes ma'am it's me, I need to talk to you about some things.

Oh, I know what you wanna know, child, everything changed once your mother died. People who had issues decided to band together to fight your mother about the territories she controlled. But, everybody wasn't happy with the split. Your mother made sure that everybody ate, but you know there is always that one bad apple or ambitious muthafucka that wants more on his plate than you've been giving him. Well, that was Dante' for your mother. She had a good eye on him and things but when he went to jail that last time, that's when your Mother thought the FEDS got a hold to his ass.

I knew it was Dante' dirty ass, but do you know what kinda deal he made?

Oh honey, there was no deal, it's much deeper than that. Dante' is a FED!!!

What did you just fuckin say to me Ms.Pat?

Yes honey, this shit is really deep, your mother was a very smart woman, she made sure that there was dirt on everybody who worked for her or with her. Never trust No One!! Remember that was her mantra.

Oh yes, mine too actually!!

So the men that have been trying to kill us are fuckin cops!! Bingo!!

Ok, thanks Ms. Pat I'll send something over to you for your help. I really appreciate it.

Ok sweetheart, tell Skye I said Hello. I will, bye!

This shit is big, way more than I thought. We need that envelope!!

As Harper is in the office handling business, Skye notices the cleaner at the front door.

Hey man

What's up ma'am? I just wanted to let you know everything has been cleaned inside and outside. Anything else I can do for you?

No, that's it, here you go and thank you again. Our pleasure, call when you need anything.

We will. We put an extra $4000 in the envelope for your very quick response and precise work.

Thank you. Have a good night ladies. You too. Bye.

Skye shuts the door behind them and takes a look around at amazement, them fools really clean, it's like nothing happened. She walks into the kitchen to make her and Harper something to eat, when her phone rings.

Hello?

Hey

Who dis?

You know who this is girl?

Ok, no time for games right now so if you're not gonna tell me who you are..

Ok, it's me..

Me who?

It's Ron girl from high school. What?

Ron, how did you get my number?

I ran into your sister a while ago and I just decided to use it. Which sister Ron?

Harper

Really? Nice hearing from you Ron. take care. No, no, Skye wai...

Skye hangs up in his face and go into the office to ask Harper if she seen this nigga anywhere?

Harp?

Yes lil sis, what do you need?

Nothing, I just got a call from Ron, from high school. He said he saw you and you gave him my number?

Yeah??

Did you give Ron my number?

No, why would I do that. I remember what he did to you girl and what the fuck we did, so no, why would i give him any info on your period?

Right? Your right sis. He just threw me for a loop, with that out the blue ass call. I'm changing my number tomorrow.

That's a good idea. I might change my shit too.

You should Harp. especially with everything that's going on.

You're right, can you actually handle that for us tomorrow? I'm setting it up to have that fool that called about this envelope that mother left us?

Yeah

Well, I think we should have him drop that off at Ms. Pat house and we have someone pick that shit up for us.

Oh yeah, I'm wit it!! If you think it's best. You've been taking care of me my whole life, no need to stop trusting you now sis.

Exactly lil sis!!

Well, I'm about to go into the office upstairs, I have some business of my own to tend to.

Ok babe, make sure you get shit together cause we're going on a trip to MIA! We gotta get some miles between us and the Bay Area at least until we find out what the fuck is really going on. It's more to this than just drugs and turf shit, this shit is deep. So get some money together and close the businesses out here for me too, please? Thank you.

You got it boo!!

Harper and Skye are both trying to figure this shit out but, they do need more evidence which seems to be in that fuckin envelope. Good thing we'll know soon. Harper sits in her mother's huge 5000 square foot office, in her all italian leather $9000 dollar chair and begins to remember what her mother always said to them, "Nothing is as it seems, always do your recon on muthafuckas and make sure that your hands are always clean!" With that wisdom swirling around in her head Harper begins to plan their next move. She needs to get them out of this situation and needs some breathing room to find out how she can to make sure Dante' pays for all the turmoil he has caused the family. It's always someone you've trusted, but I got something so cold for this nigga though, as she is sitting there she gets a call from her best friend Tanika "T" Bailey. They have been friends since the second grade, shit she was pretty much the only girl mother would let me hang around in the hood. Mother went to school with Tanika's mom so that's how we started kicking it.

Hello?

What up bitch?? Ah ha got your ass huh? Bitch where the hell have you been?

Girl, after mother's funeral I had to get some distance from the Bay girl, I ended up in South America, you know bumming around kinda just sight seeing and catching my breath girl, I couldn't believe that shit, not Mother ok. So you know, how are you babe? I just heard about Jill, I'm so sorry baby, I got back as soon as I could.

It's good, I understand. Anyway, where are you at now? I'm at my mom's house selling it actually.

It's about time girl, it ain't like you were gonna live there anyway. I know, I just wasn't ready to let it go yet.

I feel you girl, I got some property to unload of mother's myself. So, what's up? I'm hearing things.

I'm sure you are. We are at the cabin right now, but we are about to head out to MIA for a couple of weeks.

Shit sounds good, we need to catch up anyway.

Cool, I'll book your ticket with ours, we'll meet you at the airport tomorrow night. I'll text you the itinerary, ok?

Ok, tell my little sister Skye I said what up? Love her. I will see you soon boo. One!

Wow, that was right on time, I hella fuckin miss that girl. Harper continues to make all the arrangements for Miami and closes up the cabin and the mansion in the oakland hills. All the proper people are contacted to set everything in motion after the girls leave. For them to be as young as they are, they are very well versed in this life. Mother taught them very well. As Harper comes out of the office and turns off the light, she sees someone walking past the window looking in and around the house. Harper grabs her pistol and proceeds towards the door as she creeps through the hallway into the living room to the front door, shutting off lights as she moves from room to room. She gets to the door and looks at the security cams to see who it is but she doesn't recognize them. The doorbell rings and she walks over to it. She looks out the peephole and he's standing right there with a package.

What the fuck is this? Harper asks herself. She opens the door quickly putting her glock in his face just as fast.

How can I help you?

I'm FED EX ma'am, I have a package for Harper Wellington. Put your damn hands down, fool, let me see.

Ok, thank you. Eh, how did you get in here? Your gate seems to be stuck and can't close. Great, thank you. Drive safe.

Harper kicks the package as it sits on the porch, it seems harmless so she takes it inside and proceeds to open it. It's a DVD with a note saying play me..

She walks over to the tv to put the dvd into the dvd player to see what's up, and to her surprise it's a video of what looks like Dante' at a strip club sitting with that cute ass cop from the scene at Jill's house. What the fuck is going on???? Omg!!

Harper is now thinking what is the next move? She has to protect her sister Skye, she's the only family she has left. After Harper looks at the DVD she must tell her sister what's up! She proceeds into the family room where T and Skye are sitting on the couch drinking some wine and laughing as usual.

What the hell yall laughing at?

Omg! Harp, T just told me about the time y'all had a whole neighborhood of girls looking for y'all when you were teenagers.

Omg! Girl, I know you ain't telling them old tales.

Yes I am Harp! This shit is our history, we owe it to our little sister to tell her how we used to run the fuckin neighborhood my nigga!!

So, where was I? Oh yeah, so me and Harp just so happen to be walking back to my house from her house and when we got there my mom came running out the house all loud talking about " some girls came around here looking for yall asses! We were like "what are you talking about?" just what the hell I said , a whole lot of girls came here looking for you and Harper. Now, what the fuck is going on Tanika?? So , we look at each other and start walking over to this bitch named Sheila house, she was my friend before I met your sister Harper but she started hating when me and Harp started getting money together, you know. Anyway, Harp remember the look on her face when she opened the door and it was us on the porch?

Do I, that ho nearly shit her pants. As soon as she opened the door I popped her right in the face.

Why? How did ya'll know it was her?

Look ladies, this is real fun strolling down memory lane and all but, we got a package from FEDEX just now and you need to see this shit.

Aww man sis, she was just getting to the good part..

Shut up fool, I got some important shit I need to tell you guys. What Harp? What's up?

Remember Skye when I called Ms. Pat the other day? Yeah, what did she say?

A whole fuckin lot!! She let me know that Dante' was extremely jealous of mom. That he set her up, and this is the fuckin shocker my nigga.. Dante' is a fuckin FED!!

What the fuck did you just say Harper?

Oh , you heard me T, he's a damn FED. more importantly i just got a package delivered from FEDEX and it's a dvd. We need to watch this shit so we can get all our ducks in a row. Skye, T y'all know there is no way mother didn't know that and I believe she found out about something Dante' did or was about to do and was going to dead the situation, he had her killed. He knew her moves, I mean he's been working for mother for like ten muthafuckin years.

As they all sat down on the couch and started looking at the footage, they all just stared with their eyes and mouth wide open. Are they seeing what they think they're seeing? Is that Dante' with that cop? WTF!!

Harp, tell me that's not that detective from the crime scene at Janelle's damn house? I wish I could but, yes that's that snake ass nigga!

Anything you want me to do Harp?

Yes T, can you roll? We need all the help we can get. Of course, where do you need me?

We need to get out of here, Skye go upstairs and pack some bags. We out!! Where are we going?

The Caymans

Ok, come on T you can help me get this shit together while Harp does what she does!

The ladies go upstairs to gather all the items they will need to go to the Caymans. They walk straight to Skye's room and continue to pack some things that were already on the bed.

T..

Yes my dear.

What the hell is going on with my family? If someone isn't dying then they're getting shot at, or in Dante's case not dying!

I know everything is really fucked up right now, but you know Harper is gonna do everything in her power to keep you safe and punish those accordingly.

I know, that's what makes me scared too, I've already lost my mother and sister, I can't lose the one person that has always been there for me. Hell, mother didn't raise me, Harp did. Mother was busy building the empire.

Now, you can't really be mad at mother because she had to make sure she made a life for you girls that she could be proud of. I mean to be all the way 100 wit you lil sis, mother was from the hood, a product of a pimp and a hoe. She was taught very early on, "You eat, or get eaten!" so give mother a little slack.

I get it T, and you're absolutely right. I know some of my mother's story but not all of it. Well, maybe when we get settled in the islands, we can answer some questions for you. Ok lil baby?

Fuck you, I told you stop calling me that shit. Girl I ain't been nobody's lil baby in a long time.

Ok, ok! I'll leave you alone for now, but you will always be my 'lil baby', hell I'm the one who gave you that name.

For real??

Yessss!! I used to always ask Harper where we are going girl and where is the 'lil baby'? Omg! I never fuckin knew that. Cool! We better get this shit packed up before Harp comes up here fussing! You know??

You ain't lying, that woman can cuss yo ass out something good, can't she? Clown the hell out of your ass.

The girls get all the bags packed and bring them downstairs to the bottom of the staircase. They were looking for Harper, they thought she was in the office but when they checked, she wasn't in there..

Harper????

BFF, where are you?

Ok, this isn't funny. With all that's going on let's split up. Cool, you got your shit on you?

Of course I do.

Now listen, Skye you go left toward the kitchen, I'll go right toward the living room area. Are you ready?

Yeah!

Alright, on three. !, 2, 3 go!!

The two go in their separate directions and as Skye approaches the kitchen with her gun in hand pointed out in front of her, she sees the back door open. She thinks to herself, Harp wouldn't leave this open or go outside if it's snowing anyway, WTF! Skye walks toward the door with her gun leading the way, takes a look outside to see if she sees anything? She calls out for her sister, Harper??? Harper???

Skye is now outside in the pitch black of night calling out for her sister, but no response. Skye goes back into the house with the notion that maybe she didn't go out, but someone may have come in...

Harper!! Yells T as she walks through the living room to the hallway and all around the first floor. T starts to walk toward the stairs when she heard a noise in the garage area.

Harp is that you girl?

T stands right in front of the door that leads into the garage, gun in hand pointed right at that fuckin door.

Skye? Skye? Fuck where is everybody? This shit is getting fuckin creepy. Alright, here goes nothing.

T heads toward the garage where she heard the noise, she reaches for the door and as she turns the knob with her nine millimeter aimed right at the door, she walks in slowly. It's very dark and she can't see shit. There is a Range Rover and a Mercedes parked in there. T starts to creep around the benz and she turns on the inferred light on her pistol and walks around to the other side of the garage where there is a door that leads outside. She sees that the door is open and there are snowy footprints leading into the garage and then into the house. T sees this and begins to turn into soldier mode. She heads back into the house following the set of footprints to see where they lead.

Skye? Harper? Where are you guys?

Next thing, all the lights go out and now the cabin is pitch black! Omg!!

What the fuck is going on, who has the balls to come up here and mess with Harper Diamond? She asks herself as she tries to navigate through the cabin. Damn, guess we about to find out.

Crash!, crash!

All of a sudden the gigantic window in the living room shatters, then the dining room windows. Glass is everywhere and T still hasn't found Harp or Skye. She heads up to the upstairs running for her life not really knowing where she's going, she stops on the second floor in the hallway to turn on her cell phone flashlight.

Come on Galaxy 7 fuckin expensive phone show me what you got.

T walks ahead down the hallway toward the rooms on that floor and the first room checks out, the second room as she peeks in she hears muffled cries. So she goes inside the room and walks around to the side of the bed. There she finds a newborn blue-nosed pitbull puppy. Tenika looked at the dog cowering in the corner whimpering, and began to clear the room. She walks over to the puppy, by this time Tenika hears Skye calling for her as she's coming down the hallway toward the bedroom.

Yes, Skye. I'm right here. Girl, check this shit out. What the fuck is that dog doing here?

Fool, I don't know?

Ya'll don't have no dogs?

Hell naw bitch, Harp and I are never really out here at this house. I haven't heard of Jill coming out here or anything, but shit, we can each use it whenever. We all have access.

What is that on its paw? Go see T.

Bitch, I can't stand you. Your ass better be glad you the baby, shit. Come here little baby. As Tenika reaches for the puppy she notices that she has a bloody note tied to her paw. Tied with a diamond bracelet, Interesting!!

Is that a note T?

Yeah, some type of letter.

Tell me that's not blood? How did a fuckin dog get in here and we not know about it? This house was locked down like fort fuckin knots, where is my sister!!!

Calm down Skye, I know you're scared, come here sweetheart.

Tanika embraces Skye to try to calm her down. She is so afraid that something terrible has happened to her sister. She has already lost her mother and middle sister, she can't lose the one person she leans on the most in life. The one who taught her everything she knows.

Fuck that read the letter T!! Alright, here goes. Dear Skye, OMG!! It's addressed to me?

Yes girl, listen! I know you're probably trying to figure out what is going on right now? Right? Well, It's simple really. Plain old jealousy really. Ok, let's get to the point. The puppy is a clue to where your sister is being held. I took Harper so I could get your full attention and because I know you girls don't do anything unless authorized by Ms. Harper Diamond. So, like good little girls, figure out the clue and you'll be that much closer to finding her!! Oh yeah, here's another little piece for you, when your parents were married, your father brought home a blue-nosed pitbull home for you girls to play with. What did your mother do with that dog? And where? Food for thought girls. See you soon!!

Signed, Friend.

What the fuck T? Who would do this?

I don't know Skye. Do you know much about when you guys were little?

No, this will be hard. Mother never told me anything about our father, I was just told he died when I was like, 2 years old.

Damn, Skye. ok there's gotta be somewhere this information will be. Wait a minute.. This bitch Harp saves everything. Let's go to her house and check everywhere. She's very sentimental, that I know about my best friend.

You're right T, let's check her house and if we don't find anything there. There is a vault at Mother's mansion in Oakland that might have some info in it.

Cool, let's hit it!!

The girls leave the villa in the Cayman Islands and hot-tale it to the Bay Area. little do they know someone is watching their every move. Tenika began to pack her things when she noticed a postcard she got from Harper letting her know to come to hang out in the Islands with Skye and I. We haven't seen each other in so long girl. Hop a flight. Harp. Tenika forgot to tell Harper she got her postcard and was so happy to hear from her, but so much happened so fast that she never got a chance to tell her, but now it seems very suspicious. How did

Harper know where I was? How come she didn't say anything about it when I got here? All these questions are making T think someone else was driving this mission, because Harp did seem extremely surprised to see me. I need to tell Skye my thoughts.

Skye!!

What?

Girl, come here.

Here I come, just getting out of the shower. I'm in my room.

What's up? You made the reservations? Not yet, check this out.

What's this?

A postcard

Yeah, but from who? and where did you get this?

I was going through packing my things and I came across this postcard, I totally forgot to mention to Harp that I got this when I was in South America, from her.

What? She didn't know where you were.

I know, that's makes me think that the person who took Harper and left that creepy ass note are the ones that sent me that postcard so I'll be here when all this goes down.

OMG!! Do you really think so?

Yes bitch, it's some freaky shit going on right now. Let's get back so we can figure this fuckin shit out and get my muthafuckin sister back.

Bet!!

The girls head to the airport to board the family jet. Heading directly to the Bay Area to get the fuckin answers to these clues, nothing like this has ever happened to the sisters before, Skye was is so scared, she doesn't want to be alone. she's never been without her sisters, ever! The attendant arrives and asks if we would like anything before we take off?

Yes child, I need a damn shot of Patron. Yes ma'am. And for you Ms. Wellington?

Yes Robin, I would like a glass of red wine, thank you. Tell the pilot we are ready to take off as soon as he's ready.

Yes ma'am.

Thank you Robin.

While the ladies are sitting there in pure silence, each probably trying to figure out anything that they may know, or some place to look. Suddenly, Skye's phone rings.

Hello?

Is this Skye?

Yes , who the hell is this?

This is the person who is causing your misery right now!! What? Do you know who you are...

Shut up and listen!! You don't have much time to talk shit! I'm listening..

You need to go to your mother's house and go upstairs to the second floor, first room on the right and there is where you will find your next clue.

What kind of game are you playing here? This is my sister's life you fuckin with!

What did we ever do to you? Who are you?

Too many questions Skye. Tick Tock, Tick Tock! Ok, ok just tell me she's ok, please?

She's fine.

Like I said before, I really hope you know who you're fucking with?

Oh, trust me. I know exactly who I'm fucking with!! Oh yeah, you bring the puppy?

Of course, I wasn't gonna leave him.

Good, I knew you wouldn't leave him behind. You always loved animals. What? How do you know..

Get here Skye. Focus! See you soon!!

OMG!! Who was that Skye? Did you recognize the voice? Bitch, I have no idea who that is, except that it was a man. What did he say?

He told me to go to Mother's house, second floor, first door on the right. What?

Yes bitch, a straight up treasure hunt. WTF!!

Fuck that, let's get this shit done and get my fuckin BFF back man!!

You're exactly right T, we are about to dead all this shit and anyone who comes in between that. I'm on some straight up murder shit baby girl!!

Matter of fact, I'ma call the squad and tell everybody to put their fuckin ear to the ground and there is a finders fee attached. Let muthafuckas know that the amount is $50k. That'll get niggas up!

You right T, you got that. I'm on it!

Harper opens her eyes and sees that she is in trouble. From what she can see, there are five men on her. Two on the door of this big ass basement with a chair in the middle of the floor with Harper in it. One man watches the house out front, one in the back and one asshole that stays in the room with her. They are not stupid, they knew to keep a close eye on her. She hadn't seen who was actually holding her, but the one that stays inside is always on the phone taking orders from someone.

They shot me up with something, I feel so fuckin drowsy.

I gotta get my head clear so I can come up with a way out of this shit! Where am I? Who is behind all this? And more importantly, why me?

These questions will get answered, trust! These muthafuckas have fucked with the wrong Wellington!!

The asshole on the inside walks towards her and asks her if she wants some water? This may be my only chance to try anything.

Drink!

What the hell is that? Water, drink now!

Fine, I need to use the bathroom!

He looks at Harper with confusion but he gives her the drink of water and decides to untie her and let her use the restroom.

Before I untie you Ms. Wellington, do you know where you are? No, where am I?

He looks at her with remorse, yet clearly angry at her privileged lifestyle he never had the chance to live. He looks very familiar, but I can't put my finger on it.

You'll find out shortly. Time has come for retribution and for the underdog to get his turn!

What kind of fuckin shakespeare bullshit is that? You sound real fuckin weird and slightly educated. What is your beef with me? Let's keep it all the way real my nigga, who the fuck is this? I'm not easily approached. How the hell did you get so close?

All answers will be given soon. We're waiting for some other guests.

Other guests? Who are you? You can call me Nathan for now.

Ok, Nathan, why don't you let me go, we can discuss this like adults. I'm sure we can come to some kind of resolution to your obvious problem or gripe you have against me.

Oh little Harper, it's not just you, it's all of you!!!

Harper looks at him with such anger and malice in her heart.

I got to get myself out of here. I know he's going to kill me so think bitch, think!! Nathan's phone rings and he is distracted for a minute and walks to the other side of the room. Harper begins to listen to try and gather any information to try and figure out what this is about, and who is really behind this. Nathan is clearly a minion working for someone, and they gotta have some real clout and money to pull something of this magnitude off.

Yes sir, everything is going according to plan. She has just awakened and of course asked questions. No sir, I did not discuss anything with her. Yes sir, see you soon sir.

Sir? So, you are not in charge! Let me speak to whoever is in charge. Now!

I'm afraid that's not possible right now, but don't worry you will.

Why did you make it seem like you were shot calling? You ain't nothing but the fuckin help! Wow!

Nathan walks over to Harper and slaps her with such animosity, it was like he knew her. As he reaches back and slaps her, Harper is able to swing her legs up and wrap them around his neck as she's sitting in the chair. Her hands are tied behind her back and now she has his neck between her legs choking the shit out of him. She makes the move and snaps his neck. Nathan falls to the floor, dead! Harper looks around to see where the keys to the handcuffs were on him. Jackpot, front pocket. Got'em!! She unlocks herself and reaches down onto Nathan's body and grabs his gun and starts looking around to see where she is and then she hears the two men outside the door knock on the door.

Nate, are you good in there? Hey, what's up?

Then the door opens slowly and when one of the men sticks his head through the door, Harper is standing behind the door waiting for him to come all the way in. He entered the room along with the other man and to her surprise it was two men she had ran off her block trying to sell their shit. As soon as they get in the men see Nathan on the floor dead and Harper not in the chair. They reach for their guns, Harper slams the door shut. He shoots them both in the knee caps, causing them to fall and drop their weapons. Harper was so quick, they didn't even see her coming. She kicks the guns across the room, and kicks them both in the face. Now, the two men are out cold. Harper starts to check their pockets for phones and info. One of the men starts to come to and Harp shoots them both in the head. She grabs all of their phones and keys. She gets out of the room and walks out to the hallway and sees the other two men and quickly steps aside a wall, they approach the room wondering why the door was opened. One of the men began calling out to the dead men in the room and as soon as they passed her she put one in their head. Now, all of the men keeping her hostage are now dead. Harper is hell bent on finding who kidnapped her. She began to explore the property, it's some kind of house that looks under construction or abandoned is a better word. All of a sudden she hears some people talking upstairs. She goes to the stairs but before going up, she decided to call her sister to let her know she was alive and ok, during all that was going on she didn't think to call her sister. So, Harper gets to another empty room to make the call when she turns on the phone to place the call, she notices a number on the phone, it's her sister Jill's number. Her heart dropped, what the fuck? Harper places the call to sister Skye.

Skye and Tenika are just landing at the Oakland Airport and Skye's phone rings.

OMG!! It's her T! Answer it fool.

Harp is that you babe?

Yes sis, it's me. Where are you sis?

We just landed at the airport in Oakland, we been putting niggas on the streets to find you. Do you know where you are?

No, some abandoned house or something, I just killed four men. Open the phone locator app on your phone sis, see if you can locate my phone.

Ok, hold on.

While Skye is doing what her sister told her to do, Tenika looks at the postcard again. Something just told her to look at it in more detail, something about when Harper said abandoned home, she remembered there was a house on the front of the postcard.

The home was the old Dunsmuir House.

Skye asks Harp if she thinks she's on the Claremont Hotel property in Berkeley? Skye asks her and Harper looks around and it doesn't look like it.

It looks like I'm in a basement or underground somewhere. It could be though, why?

That's what was on the postcard I was sent.

Harper begins to look around and all of a sudden she gets a memory of her childhood and sees her dad, Tenika and herself here when they were kids on a field trip.

I think so T.

We got you, we are coming squad up! Hold on boo, we're coming!!

Harper walks around the basement or underground fuckin railroad or whatever the fuck this is. For some reason she thinks she's been there before, as she walks around she notices that there is some kind of tunnel. There's noise above her, she pauses for a minute, footsteps, someone's coming. She hides behind a stone wall and a man comes walking by, she recognizes him, who is that? She reaches for the gun in her back, raises it in front of her and steps out from behind the stone wall and calls out to him.

Hey?

The man freezes in place. Turn around, slowly!

The mysterious dark figure turns around slowly as she instructed him to do and to her surprise, it was her ex. Fuckin Julien Green.

JuJu is that you?

After ten years, I guess you wouldn't really recognize a brother. Especially after all we've been through.

Are you fuckin serious right now? What the hell are you doing here? Are you in on this shit?

What do you think? Can I let my hands down now?

No, you know I don't trust your ass as far as I can throw you.

Walk over there in the light.

Still bossy I see!

Harper shoots him in the leg. Owww!!

And still a hell of a shot. Sit the fuck down. Give me your phone.

Why? Why did you shoot me? Just do it!

Julien throws the phone across to her. Harper turns it on and notices the same number, Jill's number!!

Why is my dead sister's number in your recent call list? I'm only going to ask you once!

Wait, wait, ok, ok I'm bleeding to death here.

Harper walks toward him with her gun and places it on his forehead.

Ok, ok, Harp. I'll tell you. They want you dead. You, your sisters, your whole operation.

Obviously asshole, who is behind all of this? I don't know?

Harper shoots him in the other leg. Oww, damn woman! Stop shooting me!

You better start answering my questions or I'm gonna do what I should've done that night.

I'm not lying, I don't know who is running the whole show. I just know where I was supposed to be and that's it.

How do you communicate?

Via text, sometimes email. I've never heard his voice. Well, how do you know it's him?

Through one of the texts sent to me he slipped up and when the instructions were given he mentioned he was leaving the gym and heading to a gentlemen's club.

Tell me everything you know!

Fine, I was contacted via text about a year ago, A year ago??

Yes, and there was no name but quite a story. I didn't know if it was true or not but, I would take any chance to get back at this family.

Anyway, when I recognized the names I jumped at the chance. I was sent a message every couple of months telling me where to be and when. Whoever this is wants to end you Harper!

They have spared no expense. It's deep pockets behind this, that's for sho!!

So, how many are there? What?

Don't make me repeat myself Julien?

Ok, ok it's about 10. 5 on the grounds and 2 on the roof the other 3 are staff in the war "room"!

War room huh? Is that where you decided to end your life? You should've known I would find out. Didn't I find out about your snake ass? Where is this "war room"?

I can't Harper, they'll kill me and my family. What do you think I'm gonna do?

Harper puts the glock to his forehead and kneeled down in front of him so he can see her eyes.

I don't give a fuck about you. Once you broke my heart and slept with my sister, you were erased! So let me make myself extremely clear..

Harper takes the gun and puts it under his chin and says to him, Speak!!!

Ok, it's just around that corner rock and up the stairs, you'll see a door. They are armed to the teeth Harp! Be careful!

Don't say my name ever again, you're not worthy you fuckin snake-ass, bitch ass, can't think for himself ass, shell of a man!

Harp begins to walk toward the stairs when she looked back and that fuckin snake slithered away.

Damn!! That's ok I'll deal with that ass later I need to get to this war room and dead this shit!!

It made her think though, who would contact the one man that broke my heart and was the worst relationship I ever knew?

Meanwhile, while Harper was pondering the thought, she heard gunshots outside somewhere. She knew her sister and T were there with the squad ready to do damage!! She runs over to the stairway leading up and runs into a thick wooden door. Locked from the other side, Harper listened closely to the door to see if she could hear any voices. She checks the door to see if it was open and it was, Harper slowly pushes the door open and raises her glock and ducks down, ducks down and rolls behind a couch. Bullets are flying everywhere.

Shit, who are these muthafuckas? Harp was thinking as she was ducked behind the couch. She raised up and shot back, one down. Harper moved around over to the rock looking wall on her right and behind the couch. As she hears the men reloading, Harper stood up and shot the one near the door in the back of the head, turning directly to his partner and shooting him in the forehead. Clean shots. Just like mother taught me!!

Harper started looking around the room at all the intel they had on her and her organization. Only this type of breach can come from within, Harper says to herself as she starts thinking about what she was seeing. Surveillance video, pictures, recordings, bank accounts, properties.

I mean too much fuckin information for anyone to have on me, period! I run a tight ship and somewhere there's a leak...

Harper, Harper! Can you hear me sister?
Yes I'm down here in somewhat of an elaborate tunnel system. Don't worry , we got you here now, are you ok?
As good as I'm gonna be. Hurry up I got some unfinished business to take care of.
Alright, the goons are here and they're canvasing the property, they're gonna find a way in Harp don't you worry babe!!
Where's my sister T?
She's right over there on the phone. We found the way in Boss!
Good go in and retrieve the package unharmed of course. Jay?
Yes Boss?
Clean house, Understand? Yes Boss, I got it!!

The goons make it inside the tunnels and as they enter they see the dirt lined walls and carved rock that you can tell were ancient in age. They make their way up the tunnel when they begin to see blood droppings leading down another tunnel. The fellas follow orders and continue ahead , they see the stairs and the large door with bullet holes all through it. Jay sends Dre back to follow the blood droppings down that tunnel they passed before,

No loose ends or surprises you feel me, says Jay.

Hell yeah shit nobody wants to deal with Ms. Wellington, says Ron Which one, says Twin?

Don't matter shit they all crazy!

The men enter the room and lead Harper out and on her way out she sees the blood droppings and stops.

He will not get away this time bitch! Anything you need Ms. W?

Later Jay, let's get out of here and figure this shit out.

ok , I instructed the guys to gather all of the intel and bring it wherever you want it Boss.

Good Jay, smart. That's gonna tell us who this is. I guarantee there's a mistake somewhere in that shit, and I will find it.. Bring it to Mothers House.

In Oakland Ma'am? No Villa in Cabo!

Yes Ma'am, see you there.

Great, the jet is fueled and ready to go, send goons ahead to check and then call me to let me know it's good and we will be right behind you.

I'll get right on that Boss.

Jay? You stay, I have a personal project for you. No problem

Sister, sister!

Yes baby, I'm ok.

You good? No injuries?

No sister, I'm straight, just so worried I wasn't gonna see you again.

You know I ain't going nowhere! It's gonna take more than some botched kidnapping to take your sister outta here baby!

That's right, Skye says as she dances over to her sister acting silly.

Girl, get serious we need to go to Cabo and find out who is behind this. I learned a few things while I was there and things that make no sense!!

What you mean sis?

Nothing, let's figure this out. We need to go to the jet and go now. I have to get out of here in order to find out what's up.

The ladies gathered themselves together and started walking to the car when Skye asks Harper,

What's up sis? You seemed more shook than you saying!

Shit, I know it ain;t being kidnapped cause we've all been down that road before. But, I'm your damn sister and I know yo ass, what else happened up here Harp?

Alright, alright you do know your big sister. Your right Skye something else did happen up there.

What? Did anyone hurt you?

No, nothing like that, that muthafuckin Julian Green was here and actually involved with me being taken!

What the fuck bitch! I knew we would run into this maggot again, why you didn't let me kill his ass a long time ago, I will never know.

I know T, you're right and now I'm paying for it but, not for long.

What happen when you saw him bitch don't just skip over that part, you ain't seen his ass since he tried to fuck Jill back in the day. You should've murked his ass then.

You are absolutely right Skye, when I saw him I was stunned but instantly angered and went straight for my shit. Pulled it out and aimed right for his fuckin head. He was so shaken, doing hella explaining, even tried to get smart, telling me whoever he's working with is the real deal and apparently there has been a breach in the organization somewhere.

Did you shoot his ass?

Yes T, I shot him in both his legs

Which is why I don't know how the hell he got away.

Wait a minute! Got away? Sis you let this nigga get the drop on you?

Shut the fuck up Skye, as I was getting intel out of his ass, he showed me what they called the "war room"!! When I turned back around his ass was gone.

Fuck!! We gotta put a BOLO out on that ass real quick! Already ahead of you T, put the twins on it!

Oooh, he done fucked up now. Them niggas are ill wit it Harp! Exactly!! They are instructed to bring him to Boss alive!!

Aww shit, that's old Harper from back in the day! Hell yeah, let's get this shit started!!

Your ass is so crazy T, can't wait to pop a cap in a niggas ass right? You know it bitch!!

The ladies get out of the car laughing and excited about what is about to transpire! War is declared on everyone at this point. Each one of them has their own skill set and snitches that will do anything to tell them info. But, each one had murder in their eyes. When they arrived at the airport to board the private jet, Harp noticed a van parked near the field by the runway.

Who the hell is that Tre'? Which is one of Harper's personal goons.

I got it Boss!!

Tre' reaches for his phone and speaks into the speaker and gives an order. Next thing you know four men were being dragged out of the van and onto the tarmac by the four men that work for Harper who were sitting in their car which was parked strategically alongside the jet and slit their throats and placed them back inside their van and drove it away somewhere. Smooth as butter.

Take care of the Boss.

Thank you Tre'. load the boxes on the plane please. Thank you babe.

No worries Boss. anything for you.

The ladies board the plane and are immediately greeted by staff and glasses of vintage wine.

Good evening Ms. Harper will there be anything special you will be needing this trip?

No, Frank. Just the usual honey . Thank you. You got it Boss.

The private jet that the girls are riding in was Harper's gift to herself for her 30th birthday. Fully staffed and gassed up at all times. She took both her sisters on a trip to a couple countries on a shopping spree that weekend, it was a wonderful time. I think that was the last time the sisters were together on a trip. The jet is equipped with two master bedrooms , a conference room and two bathrooms with jacuzzi tubs and a gym. A perfect place for the ladies to sit down in a secluded and relaxing atmosphere.

I have always loved this plane sis.

I know Skye, anything happens to me it's yours boo, I told you that.

Yeah, and I told yo ass don't talk like that. I'm not losing another sister!!

I'm sorry babygirl, you know what I mean.

Ok, let's find out who the fuck is trying to take down our family!

You got babygirl, let's hit it. Here are all the papers and

pictures, disks, recordings and cctv stuff. We have a long night ahead, but we can stay up here as long as we like and go wherever we want, so let's get started.

First, Frank please put on some coffee and espresso please, thank you.

No worries Boss.

Alright ladies, T you take the pictures and the CCTV stuff and see what you come up with, Skye you take the recordings from the phone calls and paperwork.

What are you going to do sis?

I'm gonna call Pat, when I grabbed Julien's phone from him I looked at his recent call list and her number was there along with Jill's...

What did you just say?

I know what ya'll gonna say but, I know what I saw. I saw it before too, on someone else's phone we took down.

Damn sis, you just now saying something? We're supposed to be in this shit together.

We are, I just needed more info before I said anything but, something fuckin fishy is going on with our late sister and these people, and with Julien punk ass showing back up at this time , it's not right!!

We're gonna figure this shit out, and when we do, there will be blood shed!! A lot!!

The flight to Cabo and all the stress free amenities that go along with that is just what the doctor ordered. I'm still feeling hella sore from all the fighting for my life thing, nothing we are not used to, just been awhile. I'm glad everyone came out unscaved and alive, but,

I have to find out what the hell Julian has to do with this? And, how is Janelle involved? So many damn questions with answers that seem to have dire consequences!!

I know exactly what needs to be done to clean all this up, I just hope it's not me having to put down someone I love. First and foremost, Julian needs to be dealt with, then, find out if our sister is still alive. I swear if Jill has anything to do with this in any way, I will put her down like the disloyal dog she is!!

As Harper is taking in all of the peace and serenity, then, she hops into gangsta mode and is ready to handle business.

Harper calls Skye and T out on the balcony to discuss what the next move is.

Sis, I don't know what fuck is going on but, I have been putting all my informant ears to the ground. Anyone who may know something or whatever, everybody knows to get back to us with the info! ASAP!!

I know sis. I appreciate you so much, I have a theory that I want to run by y'all real quick...

Yeah harp, says Tenika What are you thinking sis?

I'm thinking that as I was looking at all those papers and some addresses and account numbers, shit was looking real familiar, What are you talking about sis?

I'm saying that Harper puts all of the contents of the envelope that we got from Mother's attorney who said that Mother left this for me to open if anything happened to her. Look at the first page Skye.. What the fuck!! This shit says that Mother was surveilling Janelle and found out that she was forming some sort of "team" of her own, it also states that Mother has photos of Janelle talking with different people who are enemies to this family, there were meetings being held in secret.

Omg!! Does this say what I think it is saying Harp?

Yep T, my sister has been trying to take over Mother's business and trying to have me murdered.

What the fuck man?

I know, where does this leave the family right? Well you guys , you know what needs to be done!!

Harp, here is a picture of Janelle meeting up with Julian Green last year about three months before Mother died. How could Janelle do this to the family?

Fuck that bitch, anybody that goes against the family gets dealt with! Period! That's how Mother ran this shit for years, shit, Janelle knows she took a big ass risk trying to take you out, knowing what the repercussions would be.

Greed sis, muthafuckas don't care about family no more, I honestly don't understand what happened, why is she doing this?

Oh shit y'all!!

What T?

Harp, Skye, do you guys realize per all this paperwork there is proof that Janelle tried to have you murdered and also the hit that was taken out on Mother, was orchestrated by Janelle!!

What did you just say?

Skye, I'm so sorry baby, but. Yes right here it shows the paper trail of the payments as well as transcripts of phone calls and text messages.

Let me see that!

Calm down Skye, you know I'll handle this with strategic and stealth precision.

It appears that to me she had to get help, Janelle is the one that had Dante' killed.

You think so Harp?

Yes T, it's the only thing that makes any sense. Dant' was Mother's right hand man. Remember, Mother always told us, in order to take over something you have to go through it!! So in my eyes, in order for Janelle to get as much info as she had, she needed inside intel. Yeah, but do you think Dant' would switch up on Mother like that? I mean she basically saved his life, you remember Dante' didn't have any parents and Mother was the one who took his daddy out.

What? I never knew that.

Yeah, Skye that's why Mother kept him so close, just in case he ever found out and was ever gonna be on some revenge shit, at least she had him close, and could probably see it coming.

I can't, I need a drink! Now! Calm down Skye, we got this

I know T, but I just found out that my sister is a conniving, backstabbing bitch! I deserve a drink.

Your right babygirl, matter of fact, make us all one. There are some decisions that need to be made right now that are gonna change things forever!

True tea BFF, I want to go back and start the countdown of muthafuckas we think that was in on this shit in any way shape or form!!

So, Janelle faked her death, so we wouldn't suspect her? Now you're getting it! Slow ass!!

Shut up Harper!

Just fucking with you boo, but, to answer your question yes and while we were on our way here, I was doing some brainstorming and that fine ass Detective Ryan, had to be in on helping her with that part, he was too much in my face and I believe he was trying to see what I knew or what I put together so far.

Makes a lot of sense, says T.

Janelle knows I'm not stupid, I have an MBA from Harvard University, Mother's money well spent.

Ok bitch, yells T with such admiration for her friend.

I say we stay here for a couple of days and regroup then on Friday make our move.

What do you think she's been doing all this time? Says T, with confusion and sorrow in her voice. T knows what needs to be done and what we're gonna have to do.

Getting ready for me!!

The ladies enjoy the Island for a few more days all the while strategizing and marking names. The ladies decide to go to dinner and they of course the best of everything, get the best VIP table.

Here you are Ms. Wellington, how nice to see you again. Thank you Tyler, and you as well. How's the family?

Oh, everyone's great.

Wonderful, can you start us off with your best champagne? Of course Ma'am, anything else before your meal?

Some appetizers will be fine.

Very good, i will return with your champagne Thank you sweetie.

The ladies enjoy dinner engaging in all kinds of conversation. It was really weird, I think no one wanted to face the fact that Janelle and Dante' are trying something scandalous.

Ok, ladies off to the villa.

Yes Harp, I am so full and a little tipsy girl.

Skye, your ass is so crazy, you always gotta make a drunk ass remark. Get in the car fool!

Ok, Boss Lady. Don't call me that!

Why? Harper, you know you have to take care of everything big sis.

Ok, someone is drunk, Harper says to Taneka. What are we going to do with her?

Nothing, put her ass in the bed, and get to work. Right, I got you .

I know you do, with all this shit going on T, I don't know who to trust.

Be easy boo, as long as I have breath, I got your back. You and your family have been there for me and mine forever. Harper without you I wouldn't be able to live the kind of lifestyle that I

Have. I can remember when we were little girls playing in the streets, well, as far as Mother would let us go. I miss her so much.

Me too, Mother would know exactly what to do right now. You do to Harp, just are you gonna do what needs to be done?

I have no problem doing anything? You know that!!

Harper goes to her room to do some preparation of her own. She knew that eventually there would be a definite showdown between two powerful women. In Harper's mind Janelle and Dante 'are involved somehow in this but, where does Julian come in. I'm sure she wanted to use whatever she had on her sister to make this string as bad as possible. As Harper sits in her room contemplating her next move she goes to the closet and opens a secret safe and takes out her "go bag". This has everything she's gonna need to do what she has to do. First things first, find out where Janelle is held up at, cause can't nobody tell me anything different, Janele faked her death to eventually kill me to become the head of the family!

I need to call Ms. pat the neighborhood rat and find out what she knows, if anybody can find out it's her. So, Harper calls Ms. Pat and questions her.

Hello, hey Ms. Pat, how are you? Harper is that you baby?

Yes ma'am.

How are you, baby? I haven't seen or heard from you in a few months, everything ok baby?

No, not really, have you seen or heard from Dante' or my sister before they were killed?

What was that baby? I didn't quite hear what you said.

I think you heard me just fine and I want you to do me a big favor, put the word out that I'm looking for info regarding any type of disloyalty or any fuckin shady shit that's been going on since I've been gone.

Harper, I don't know what you're talking about, you know always give you any info I hear.

Yeah, I think you do. I'll tell you what I'll be over to visit you soon.

Ugh, ok Harper stay sweet baby.

Harper didn't even say goodbye. She never had to be rude to Ms. Pat before but, she knew, don't shit happen in the hood without her ass knowing about it. Plus, she is on the fuckin payroll. For now!!! Harper packs a few things and heads for the stairs, when she peeks in on her sister and in that moment she knows she may not see her again, as she gazes at the young woman she's become, she realizes that she has to live if not for herself than for her sister Skye. She has no one left. Our father has been out of our lives for some years now, he and Mother were together for about twenty-three years. Dad didn't want to lead the life anymore and so Mother set him up somewhere in another state but always kept tabs on him, just in case. He has a business and a pretty good life because of Mother. I think she respected the fact that he didn't cheat or go out like a snitch, he came at her real respectful and was honest. So, like the fuckin Boss she was she made sure he was cool after all he gave her us! her prized possessions. Skye was just a baby when he left, so she doesn't know him. I always knew one day she would have questions but, so far, nothing. Harper closes the door ever so quietly not to wake her sister because she knew she would not let her do what she was about to do.

As she picks her bags up and heads downstairs to go into the kitchen, T turns on the light in the living room as Harper creeps by.

And, where are you off to?

You know T, I gotta handle this myself, I have one sister left and I know her like the back of my hand. Yes, we all know the rules of the family but, she would never get over what I have to do. Now, don't get me wrong T, I know you got my back but, I wouldn't forgive myself if anything happened to ya'll, you're all I have left.

I hear you babe, promise me you'll be careful? Of course, you know how I do!

I sure do. And, I pity whoever is in your scope cause your a hell of a fuckin shot!! Bitch!

Tenika watches her friend drive off in her M6 BMW. T knows that she needs to listen and trust her friend but she had a feeling in the pit of her stomach that was gnawing at her. She knew it time to put the baby to sleep and she knows Harper better than she knows herself sometimes and Tenika feels like Harper is going to be in a fucked up position when she comes face to face to who has been doing this shit. Especially if it's who thinks who she thinks it is. T goes upstairs to Harper's room to try to find out where she was headed but nothing.

So, T picks up her phone to put some feelers out there and a BOLO for Dante' and Janelle.

Hey yo! What's it looking like out there? T is that you boo?

Clearly, look I need you to get on some shit for me Tre'

Alright, calm down and tell me what happened? Where is Ms. Diamond? That's what I'm calling about she left us here and went rogue nigga!

What?

Yes, Harp thinks she knows what's going on and who's trying to kill her? Who? I put the muthafucka down right now!!

I know you will baby, listen. Get the squad up and wait for my call. Peace. Bet!

While Tenika is in the office making calls she notices the paperwork that we found at the Dunsmuir. She started to read it and the look on her face was sheer horror. The things that have been going on behind Mother's back and Harper's. The utter betrayal will destroy this family forever. Inside one of the folders, T can see that Dante' and Janelle have been in for at least the last several years. There's bank statements, ledgers, passwords to computer files, all we need to nail they're ass! Oh shit, she says to herself as she sees pictures of Janelle and Julian together in many different places and clearly planning something. I remember when Harper first started dating that fool. She was head over heels for some Julian Green. They lasted a long time, ten whole years. We all thought they were going to get married but, Ju Ju head fucked up! Harper took full care of this nigga and he had the nerve to cheat on her and steal some of her money out of her safe. Bitch went ballistic, this muthafucka knew how she would do anything for him cause she has bailed him and his family out of so many binds and problems. No one could believe that he would snake a bitch like that.

Especially since he had the privilege to be with a Diamond, tripping! Anyway, once Harper found out everything she came home from work to kick his ass out and he was gone... disappeared! We went on to look for him and I found him hiding out in Texas. I called Harp to let her know what I found and she flew the family jet straight where this bitch was and the plan was to go and make him pay but she saw how pathetic he was and gave him a reprieve. Niggas just don't know when to quit.

T puts all the paperwork in some type of order and watches every video, she now knows everything Harper knows, time to go to war!!

Skye baby! Time to save our sister.

What are you talking about girl, my damn head is killing me. You drank your weight in champagne last night, crazy girl.

Oh lord, I feel it now. What's all this stuff T? And, where is Harper still sleeping? No, she left Skye. What do you mean she left? She needs us.

I know, I feel the same way but, you know how she is she doesn't want to lose anyone else she said.

Wait, so you saw her and didn't stop her?

Stop her, bitch are you still drunk, Have we met? Lol! You can't stop that lady from doing anything she puts her mind to.

Ain't that the truth! So I know yo ass got a plan, what are we doing?

First sit down here so I can tell you that we think it's Janelle and Dante' behind this whole thing. Look at all the paperwork that was taken from the old house when they kidnapped her. It shows all the players, what is planned and who is behind it all. Look for yourself.

Wtf!! This is so scandalous. I can't believe that our own sister is doing us dirty. Actually, I can. Says T.

What do you mean T?

Your sisters have always been in competition since they were kids. At least that's what Janelle thinks, Harper loved her sister to death both of y'all. She'll do anything for the vitality of this family. She always understood the importance of The Family.

Yeah, I hear you T but, if we lose her, then what? I can't live without her. Fuck this shit man. We bout to get it poppin right fuckin now!

Skye grabs her phone and calls her goons.

Yo nigga!

What up Ms. Diamond?

I need you to find my sister Harper and assist where needed, understand? Understood Ma'am!

Good, now go make me proud! Got you, One!

Skye hung up the phone and began looking at all the papers all over the office desk. She took a special look at anything that pertained to Julian Green. What was he doing? Why does he want to fuck with Harper Diamond?

This nigga is asking to die! T, let's hit boo.

Where will we start?

Ms. Pat. I know everything that goes down in the hood, we need to see what she knows.

Ok, Skye. you know I'm wit you. Let's be smart and stealth. Goes without saying.

I'm just saying I know you are a hothead and all, I just don't want anymore bloodshed baby girl.

Well, this ain't for you then. Niggas is bout to die!!

The girls leave the villa with a plan in action and revenge in their hearts.

Skye was not about to lose her sister to this nothing ass nigga Julian, his jealousy was so unbelievably stupid, my sister gave him everything and he fucked her, not only does he gets to keep his life, but he ran away. Now, why are you here, and to top it all off you and my sister Janelle got the nerve to hatch a plan together against my baby Harper, Guns blazing is all I understand right now. As the ladies approach the airport, they see a bunch of US Marshalls outside the terminal. They were standing there talking to people as they boarded. Weird.

The girls board the plane and as they go down the aisle to first class, Skye notices a familiar face.

Well hello Michael, How have you been all these years?

Skye Diamond as I live and breathe. Girl, how are you doing? Come give your uncle some love.

Skye , who is this fool?

T, don't worry he is cool. This is my father's brother.

Your father's brother, I never knew your father had a brother.

Right, we didn't know either. I met him when I was about sixteen. He came to my club in Vegas one night and as I walked in the door, stopped me and said I think you're my niece. I was like, nigga please.

You got me mixed up. And, he said No, is your father's name Ray Wilshire?

Yes, how do you know my father? And that's when he told me he was my dads brother, and we've been cool ever since.

So, uncle Mike, where are you off to?

Actually, the Bay Area. I got some business I need to attend to. Where are you lovely ladies headed to?

Home baby, just had some relaxation to get and now we gotta get back to the grind, you know how it is!

For sho. I was so sorry to hear about your Mother and your sister. Thank you, it's the way shit goes you know? Gotta keep moving though. I know but, you keep your head up. You call me if you need anything.

I sure will. Love you uncle. Talk to you soon.

The ladies took their seats and began talking through the plan. So where's the first stop?

Ms. Pat, you still high bitch? Damn.

Shut yo ass up girl.LOl I'm good. Just staying on track, fool.

Cool, when we land, let's head straight to Mother's to grab some essentials and go to work. You ready for this Skye?

What are you talking about bitch? This ain't my first rodeo.

I know that but, this time the targets are family, it's different.

Not, according to my Mother. "If they fuck you and you didn't spread your legs, you end them. There will be no raping of my fuckin girls ever"!!

Can't disagree with that.

Skye looked at Tenika in her face and knew the Beast was in!! Which was good cause I was beginning to question this bitches heart. Is she still up for this shit or what? But, T never disappoints. The plane has now landed at the Oakland Airport and the limo is waiting and our bags are in the car.

Let's hit it T, a lot of work to do. Alright here I come.

The girls get into the limo and head straight to Mother mansion. It always looked scary, especially at night. All white, huge Oak trees everywhere, expensive cars in a rounded driveway. Beautiful but if you knew who lived there, it's scary. Anyway, as the ladies exit the limo the driver is unloading the bags and carrying them into the house. Skye walks upstairs to her bedroom and immediately changes into her beast mode gear, taking bitch head off attire. T went into the guest bedroom and did the exact same thing. The woman knew what they were about to do and was not scared or gave a fuck what it was, it was on period!

They met downstairs in the basement where there was an arsenal that would impress any hitman or gangsta around. Mother did not play, she was prepared for anything and anyone. Uck the bullshit, you come here incorrect, she will correct you, quickly.

Aight T, grab what you know you can use and anything you think we might need. Omg, look Skye, Harper's been here.

How do you know girl?

Look this is her favorite ring, it's the one she bought herself after Julian broke her heart, he was supposed to buy it but they didn't make it that far. She wore this around her neck with a beautiful diamond necklace.

You're right Tenika. She's been here, look Mother's pearl-gripped .45 is missing. Ok, let's go find my fuckin sister. You got everything?

Yep!

Let's hit it!

The girls jump into the range rover, it's black and really tinted windows. Skye drives with malice in her eyes and vengeance in her heart. T is in the back seat loading everything when her phone rings.

Hello?

Hey T this is Tre' I found Ms. Diamond, she just left a business over by the coliseum. Do you want me to continue to tail her?

Yes, do not let her know you're following her please, and do not intervene unless absolutely necessary, understood?

Yes Ma'am, I got it.

Great, call you in a minute.

Skye, let's get to Ms. Pat. I have a feeling my friend is on a rampage and she's gone completely mad.

When the ladies arrive at Ms. Pat's home they see that all the lights are off. Everyone knows that Ms. Nosey Pat never turns that back dining room light off ever, so they already knew something was wrong or different. They get out of the car and approach the porch, when Skye notices a shiny something on the steps, she bends down to pick it up and it turns out to be a necklace with a name on it .

T, look.

What is it Skye?

It's Ms. Pat's necklace Mother gave her when she first started working for the family.

Keep it, let's see what the hell is going on here T, Ms. Pat? Are you home boo?

There was no answer, so the girls proceed through the house and it's dark and there is that smell that you cannot deny, you know it if you've ever smelled it before. T goes into Ms. Pat's room and finds her in bed with a bullet in her left temple.

Skye?

Yeah, where are you at?

In the bedroom, Harper's been here!!

Skye runs to the back of the house to Ms. Pat's bedroom and as she comes in she says, what are you talking about omg!! What happened? Oh Ms. Pat, who did this to you sweetie?

Your sister?

What did you just bitch? My sister wouldn't kill her without a very good fuckin reason.

I know Skye, I told you this journey was about to be a dark one. The shit we're about to find will fuckin blow your mind. But, I know Harper like the back of my hand and she knew that we would follow so I think the info she needed from her, Ms. Pat didn't tell the truth. Remember no one knows that Harp has paperwork with names and dates. Muthafuckas is in for a rude awakening, she ' "'s in rare form Skye!

What do we do about Ms. Pat? We can't just leave her here.

Yes the fuck we can and we will, call the cleaner and we need to find Harper Now!!

Harper is sitting at the red light going over in her mind about what just transpired between her and Ms. Pat. she went there with the intent to speak with Ms. Pat but when she pulled up, there were some men outside she had never seen before. Harper took the other way to the house just in case she was being followed. Good thing too, that's when she saw the two BMWs parked around the corner from Ms. Pat house. Harper knows everyone on that block. The Diamond Family owns most of the homes on that block and actually Mother bought a whole grid of Oakland property, so that low income people can stay in their homes and so she can watch her business. So, when Harper pulls around the corner she knows when shit looks different. She parks across the street from the neighbor of Pat's house and gets out the car in all black attire, black beanie, 3 inch heel boots and two nine millimeters in her back. She walks across the street going into the house next door. The men watch her as she walks into the home with keys.

Hello fellas. Nice night.

Sue is sista. How are you doing? Good boys, real good.

Harper gets inside the house and walks downstairs to the basement and opens a secret passageway built in case myself or any of my sisters were ever in the house and the FEDS hit. Harper looks around at how nothing in the house has changed. No one has lived here since my uncle died fifteen years ago. We kept it due to the tunnel system through the hood. She climbs up a ladder to open the cutout in the ceiling for the remote to open the door. No one knows of this as far as any of the employees, loose lips, sink ships! Tupac wasn't lying. The door opens and Harper climbs down from the ladder and walks through with the door shutting behind her. Moving cobwebs out of her face she pulls her pistols out and points them in front of her. She gets through the initial part of the tunnel and the next turn is the inside of Ms. Pat's kitchen pantry. Harper knows by now that Ms. Pat knows she on to her, I'm sure that's why she thought she could call these amateurs to deal with her. Huh, this old ho need a lesson in loyalty. Harper opens the door to enter the pantry. She can hear people talking so she waits patiently for the perfect time to make her move. After forty minutes or so, Harper got impatient, she went back down to the tunnel to find the breaker box, she put the silencer onto the gun and shot the box to knock out the power. In pure darkness she a fuckin ninja, Harper went on a retreat in Japan and came back with all kinds of skills to kill a muthafucka, stealth mode.she taps into her training and maneuvers around the house like a ghost. She comes out of the pantry and she can hear a nigga in the kitchen, she grabs him by the neck and snaps it like a twig in five seconds. You know a bitch was top of her class, come on! She moves quietly through the house listening for any movement. She hears the other guy near the back door, she puts two in him from ten feet away in pure darkness. Harper ducks down behind a couch when she hears another one coming in through the front door, as he crosses the living room looking for her, she lays on the floor on her back and aims upward and puts two in his head. As his body drops Harper can hear a gasp from Pat.

Oh, Ms. Pat, is that you honey? Did you think I wasn't coming prepared?

What do you mean Harper? Those are my nephews.

Stop fuckin lying man, and where is all the stuttering coming from?

What do you have to tell me Pat?

I swear I don't know what you're talking about!

Sshhh, calm down. Have a seat. I think you know exactly what I'm talking about, I'm so sure of it I came prepared for you tonight. See I know when I called you and told you that I was coming to talk to you about some shit I'm hearing and, when I brought up Dante', you did that stuttering shit then too.

Harper please, I'm an old woman. I just do what I'm told, you know that.

Right , and who do you work for? The Family.

Yes, but who do you ultimately work for? Don't fuckin play wit me right now.

Ok, ok, you're right you do take extra care of me to do the things you need done. But, Harper, I didn't know that they were serious.

Who?And, serious about what?

Well, one day Janelle and Dante' came by here to do some business and they were discussing a meeting you guys had about shutting down the business.

And!!

Harper is sitting across from Pat with evil in her eyes. She staring her down with the pistol on the table in front of her.

And, they seemed to be trying to come up with a plan to get you out of the way so they can run the business together.

What? My own fuckin sister, and Dante' i expected more from his ass. But, it's all good, I got something for that ass. What else?

Well, the last thing I heard was Dante' was on his way to Vegas to handle something and Janelle said she would handle shit here. Harper I wanted no part in this but they told me they would kill me! Pat says crying trying to appeal to Harper's good nature.

Thank you Ms. Pat, you helped me a lot this evening. What's gonna happen to me Harper?

Shhh, everything will be fine. Harper tells her as she stands behind her as she sits in that chair, Harper puts her hands on Pat's shoulders to calm her. She grabs Harper's hand and says Oh thank you Harper, I knew once I explained everything to you would understand.

Of course, yes let's recap shall we.

Harper starts to squeeze Pat's shoulders to show her disappointment in her.

I know you paid some fools to take me out upon my arrival here.

I did.

Harper leans in to whisper to her in her ear, I knew you would try something, that's why I came the way.

So, what happens now? I told you everything I know, I swear Harp!!

Calm down, you'll raise your blood pressure. You don't wanna do that, with your health, I mean I know, I pay your fuckin medical bills. As she slaps Ms. Pat in the face.

Harper gathers any shell casings and walks toward the pantry to go back through the tunnel when she looks back at Ms. Pat sitting at the table reaching for her phone,

You never let me down Ms. Pat.

Harper walks back over to her and looks her dead in her eyes and puts the gun to her temple and before she could whimper anything, Harp put two in her head and she then proceeded to just lay her head down on the table. Harper moves fast through the tunnel to get back to her car quickly. She reaches outside and as she comes out of the house next door, the same guys are on the street now in front of the house. As Harper walks out the gate and walks across the street she can feel someone following her. She turns around very quickly.

Can I help you?

Whoa, you fast. Just wanted to say hello, you are gorgeous.

Well thank you. Harper replied as she put her bag in the car.

Where you headed tonight baby?

I wanna be where you at! He says laughing at himself I guess he calls that game.

I have some business to attend to tonight but maybe another time.

You sure do baby, cause you look like you just took care of some business with that nice, tight ass, black ninja outfit you got on.

Oh, you got jokes, ok. Take care now.

Ok sweet thang. You be safe out here. Watch out for them creeps out there.

Honey, they better watch out for me! You have a good night.

Harper pulls off in the black Range riding down the street

thinking about her next move. Something Pat said made her think, she said Janelle and Dante' was planning something, that got Harper thinking of her sister and getting into her mind. One thing Harper knows is the level of Janelle's jealousy of her. The light turns green and as she driving to her house in Castro Valley she notices the red and blue lights behind her,

What the fuck is this shit? Harper is pissed but she cooperates and pulls over. The police pull up behind her and get out, walk around the car and come to the driver side window.

Hello Ma'am, did you know that you have a tail light out? No, I did not officer. I will get it fixed immediately.

I'm sure you will Harper Diamond.

Excuse me! How do you know my name sir? I knew your Mother.

Ok, and that has what to do with me? Oh, are we getting smart Miss?

No sir, it's just late and I'm ready to go home and relax. Ok, you drive safe and stay out of trouble Ma'am.

I will sir, have a good night officer.

Harper drives off thanking God she didn't have to deal with that shit, she has a plan to execute. Back to her sister, when harper went to Janelle's house and saw her dead body on her bathroom floor, she realized she didn't look at her whole body. Mother always told us if there is a kidnapping or a death, we can tell its us through our tattoos. We each got a three diamond tattoo on the inside of our wrist when we each turned sixteen, kind of like a family branding. Janelle instructions in her will per her burial wishes, they were not like ours. We're all going to be buried in the Mausoleum with Mother. But, Janelle changed her Will about a year ago and I didn't know anything about it. As Harper's riding and thinking of how the pieces are starting to fit she drives to Janelle's house to see if there is any paperwork she could find to make sense of all this crazy shit. Harper pulls into the garage and starts to tear up at what she knows will be this bullshits end game. She goes in the house through the garage and it's so dark and quiet. She has some thoughts about some of the memories they shared. She shaked that shit off and headed straight for Janelle's room. There is a safe made into the floor, let's see what's in it, shall we?

As Harper begins to look through the paperwork she comes across surgery consent forms and receipts for plastic surgery. Harper's wheels start to spin and she now has to go and see for herself, who is buried in that damn plot. Harper jumps into her car and makes a b line for the Cemetary. On the way, she calls some of the lower level goons, goons trying to make their way up the ladder. I knew they're so hungry, they'll do anything.

Hey, it's me. I need you to get over to the cemetery where my sister was buried.

Bet, you good Boss? What do you need?

I'll tell you when I arrive, bring some shovels with you too.

I will be soon, just get here ASAP!! Keep it on the low.

On my way.

Actually bring about four. Thank you, boo. Don't keep me waiting.

I won't Ms. Diamond.

As Harper arrives at the cemetery, she begins to think of her Mother. Instantly, she teared up thinking about how the Family has changed. Mother would be so disappointed in what has transpired between my sisters and I.

Harper decides after she parked her car, she needed to see her Mother. Harper knew what she would have to potentially do requires her to be the woman her Mother raised. So, she goes to talk to her Mother. She hadn't been there since the funeral, kinda weird without this lady here to fix everything.

Mother, I think we have a trader in our midst of the highest betrayal. I'm doing everything you taught me Mother, I am feeling some type of way about what I know I gotta do in order to keep this family intact. You're right I just need to follow my instincts and I can't go wrong. I love you Mother, I know we had unresolved business between you and I but, I guess it wasn't that important after all.

Harper lays against the marble stone that Incaste her Mother's glass casket. Crying and feeling so alone in that moment, Harper took the time to be a daughter and she could feel her Mother's arms around her in that very moment giving her the comfort she needed to go on. Harper gets up off of the floor and dusts herself off. It's time to go to work!

She pulls her phone out and calls her blank face,
Hey, y'all ready/
Ready when you are Boss, and we have a surprise for you too.
A surprise? What kind of damn surprise could you have for me?
Don't worry Boss, Trust, Bbbby stares at the trunk of his car at what he had for his Boss with great admiration in his heart. You're gonna love this.
Ok, come around, I'm coming out of the Mausoleum.
Bet, on the way.
Harper walks out of the Cript with the spirit of her Mother walking with her. As Harper enters the fresh air she looks to her left and there they were, waiting for her, just like good boys. She knew what she had to ask them to do and that these were the type of niggas that put in that work. They gives no fucks! Just like me!!
Hey fellas, everything good?
Great Boss, especially when you see what I have for you.

That's Bobby, he's been trying to move up for a minute now. He put in good work, and he mad loyal, just what a bitch needs right about now. I like his style and maybe somebody will be getting a promotion tonight? We'll have to see what's this fuckin surprise.

So, Bobby. What kind of surprise could you have for me? You know, you took a big risk going on your own and doing something I did not instruct you to do, right?

Yes Ma'am, but since I know the situation of The Family, and my loyalty lies with The Family always, I took it upon myself to take care of something for you.

I appreciate that. Why don't we do what we came here to do and you can surprise a bitch later! Ok?

Yes Boss, of course. Where do you need us?

Right here, I need y'all to dig out my sister's Crypt so I can open her casket, any questions?

No , not at all. Get the shovels yo, let's get to it man.

The soldiers walk inside and begin to do just what they were instructed to do. As they are working on the task at hand, Harper is standing over near the tree where her and her sisters had a marble bench installed for when they come to see their mother. She sits there in the dark watching everything. All of a sudden the trunk of Bobby's car starts making noise. What the hell is Bobby up to now? If Mother was alive, he wouldn't live past tonight. Due to the fact that he took it upon himself and went to do whatever he did, Mother doesn't like her soldiers thinking on their own about shit. You follow instructions and do what you're told. Period! But, I kind of like a nigga that can take a little initiative and get some things done without a bitch always having to hold your hand on some shit.

And what would that be?

Well, take a look. Open the trunk man.

As he put his hand on that trunk, Harper already had her hand around her back on her pistol. As Bobby hits the remote to unlock the trunk, Harper prepares herself just in case these niggas get some courage right now, the trunk opens.

Inside is Julian's punk ass. Lord knows Harper wanted to find his cowardly ass and fast. She knew he knew more than he told her, clearly, otherwise why would he run. Harper was thinking to herself as she watched him squirm in that trunk, she should've let her fuckin cousins take care of his ass a long time ago when he hurt me. But, no I gotta be a damn 'capitan save a nigga', this fool wouldn't even be a factor. Love makes you do stupid shit!!

Where did you find him?

I got a call from a friend of mine and he let me know that this mothafucka was at his sister's house hiding out, he said he was shot in the leg and needed a doctor but a doctor that would come to the house. That's when she called me, when I asked her who this shit was for, she told me. Now, I know from keeping my ear to the street that you put it out there that you wanted him brought in alive! So I took my opportunity.

I see. Close the trunk. Hey! Heyyyy!!

Shut up nigga! You're gonna get out, don't worry.

Look, leave this piece of shit here and let's continue with the task, y'all got the casket open yet?

Yep, just waiting for you Boss. Ok, let's see it.

The five of them walk over to the wall where they have dug out Janelle's casket, I can't believe I'm about to do this. Harper looks inside, she looks as if she just died, wow! Lord, let me be wrong. As Harper grabs her sister's arm to turn it over so she can see the inside of her wrist, there was no tattoo. Harper jumps back away from the casket. She grabs her chest and stands there shaking her head.

What the fuck yo?

What up Boss? What are you looking for?See Don't worry about it, I found it. That's what's important. Let's go.

Where are you headed to Ms.Diamond?

I have something I need to take care of, you guys meet me at my house in 45 minutes. Understood?

Yes Ma'am.

Oh yeah, bring the surprise with you. No problem Boss.

Harper headed to her storage facility in Hayward. When she arrives, she opens the gate with the remote and drives in. She turns a corner to head to her unit, when she sees three guys standing in front of another unit about forty feet away. They seem to be harmless but she couldn't help but notice it was awfully late at night, but Harper had bigger fish to fry. That's just my damn spidey sense kicking in. She opens her unit and walks in shutting the door behind her. She hits the remote in her pocket to separate the walls where she holds an arsenal of whatever kind of fire power she needs. Harper changes her clothes, throws on a black tracksuit and grabs her favorite gun of all, 'Shelby'! Her custom-made, chrome hand grip and silencer, also she grabs some .45's, a couple of grenades, AK-47 w/ scope action, binoculars, and an shit load of ammunition. Harper now knows her sister is behind all this in some way, but she didn't do it alone. Harper leaves the unit and loads the car with all of her toys. As she pulls out of the facility, she makes a call.

What up man? I need a favor.

Of course you do, don't you always harp?

Fuck you. Don't I pay your bills? You little shit. Where are you at right now? Handling some business, what's up?

I need you to meet me at my house in Castro Valley in about 20 minutes. Ok, what do you need, Boss?

You don't wanna know, but I'll fill you in later, 20 min man. I'll be there, you alright Cuz?

Fo sho, see ya. Bet.

Harper drives towards the freeway to head home. She stops to get some gas and an officer is inside getting some coffee. She walks in with no qualms about her, Harper doesn't scare easily and she's been dealing with cops all her life. She grabs a cole and tells the cashier to put 80 on pump 2.

No problem Ma'am, and how are you doing this evening? I'm well, thank you. Take care.

Goodnight ma'am.

Harper starts to pump her gas and she hears her phone ringing, when she gets in the car to look at it, it's T. I can't talk right now T, but I know you and Skye are somewhere on my heels. She closes her phone ignoring the call. She hears the pump click, she hangs up the nozzle and gets back in the car and heads straight for the freeway. She gets off at her exit after about 10 minutes. She gets stopped by the light. As she's waiting there, the red and blue lights come on everywhere. They surround her from all sides.

Harper Diamond! Step out of the vehicle and put your hands on your head!

Harper sits in her truck for a minute thinking about what's in her trunk, what the hell do they want with me? So, she gets out with her hands up.

The closest officers come grabs her by her hands and whips them around her back, he then puts the cuffs on her.

What is this about? And I need to speak to someone in charge, now! Do you have any idea who I am, you simple bastards?

Why, yes we do Ms. Diamond. We have some interesting information that we wanted to ask you about.

And, you couldn't pick up a phone Detective?

Yea, but i didn't want to, I'm sure you are used to things going a different way for you when you're in this kind of predicament. Am I right?

No, because I don't get into these kinds of predicaments as you call them. Is all this necessary Detective? I'm sure we can work out any misunderstandings you may have in the morning at your office maybe?

Well, I guess so. I'll be watching you harper. Know that! Yes sir. Thank you. You boys stay safe tonight.

The officer takes the cuffs off and she gets in her car and leaves. Harper is sweating bullets on the way home wondering what the hell that fuckin detective wants to talk about. Anyway, back to the task at hand. She pulls into her eight car garage home in the beautiful hills of Castro valley. She walks around to the trunk and begins removing her toys and putting them in the soundproof basement.

When she comes back upstairs she headlights pull up. Great, right on time. She opened the garages and the cars went inside.

Ok, fellas, please bring your surprise down to the basement please. Thank you.

No problem Ma;am.

Put him in the chair please.

The men sit Julian in the chair that was put in the center of the room. He still had a cloth bag over his head and he is tied up with both hands and feet. Harper walks up behind him and whispers in his ear, do you know where you are Julian?

I do now. What are you gonna do to me harp? I didn't do anything.

Shut up with all that whining. You're going to tell me who hired you, and who is trying to take over my family's empire?

I can't, they'll kill me.

Ha, ha, Harper laughs along with everyone else in the room. Nigga, if you don't tell me what I want to know in a timely manner, I'm going to kill you.

You wouldn't do it Harp, you know you still love me.

Oh my word, this nigga done hit his head one to many times i think.

Do you really think that I love you Julian Green? After all you've

done to me and what I think you're doing now, I will end you and not miss a wink of sleep about it, so let's get down to business shall we?

Boys, bring me my toys please, they are over there in those cases. Thank you. Here is your fee.

Wow, 20 G's for a few hours of work. That's what I'm talking about Boss. you the real deal!

You're absolutely right Bobby. Now, let's get some information.

I don...

Please do not insult my intelligence. I know whoever is trying to take me out, you're working for them. Even though I know, if I wanted to end me, you know most of my secrets, I admit that. But, that was then boo, everything has been changed. All passwords, accounts, combinations, everything i could think of that your scandalous ass might use, so don't play with me. Who do you work for?

I can't Harp!

Ok, Harper proceeds to shoot him in the knee. Remember anything now, No? She shoots him in the other knee.

Stop playing with me Julian, I will kill you right here and bury you right under my dining room window where I can look out at you everyday as I'm having my morning coffee! Understand me?

Yes!!

Good. Now, who do you work for? You're bleeding kinda bad so, you should say something soon, before you bleed out.

I understand your angry Harp. but, you gotta know, I would never do anything purposely to hurt you. I was told if I didn't go along, they would kill my whole family. Harp please!! Julian yells as he pleads for his life.

Who are they Julian?

I told you I can't tell you that! I swear! I didn't do anything but drop off some paperwork at a few places and show my face somewhere so that you would spot me somewhere.

So , whoever you work for is playing a sad game of chess?

Ok, cool.

What's gonna happen to me? I told you all I know Harp!

Harper gets real close to his face and tells him in her most sinister voice.

You got one more time to call me that and I will disembowel you right here!!

Call you what Harp? I've always called you that.

What did I tell your disloyal ass? Is that all you have to say Julian?

I don't know anything else.

Good, I was hoping you would say that.

Harper grabs his head and pulls in back exposing his neck to the room as she slices his neck from ear to ear! Blood splatters all over her face, she feels the warmth of his blood on her neck. It reminds her of how warm he used to make her feel when she gave him all her love. She looked over at Bobby and he and the other boys were in shock at what Harper just did in front of them. She snaps her fingers at them as she wipes the blood off of her.

Hey, wake yall ass up!!

The boys are staring at Julian like they ain't never seen a dead body before.

Ya'll muthafuckas alright?

Yes Boss, we're good. Just never seen it, always heard about it from the streets but, you know, to see it for yourself is amazing!

Seen what?

We all knew you were a bad bitch boss but, damn! You are!!

Great, now you know nigga! Bobby

Take the trash out. I'm gonna call the cleaner. I got you Boss.

Thank you Bobby, for all your help. We'll talk soon. Great. Looking forward to it.

Good. go home and get some rest. Oh, when y'all picked that rat up, was he driving anything?

Yes, a BMW black with peanut butter interior.

Good, wipe it down and clean it out of everything. Anything you find, bring to me. Got it?

Yep, got you Boss.

Alright, get outta here. I got business to take care of.

Skye and T are pulling up to Ms. Pat's house. It looks dark in there. You think she is home Skye?

T, where is her old ass going at three in the morning bitch? Come on. I bet you anything my sister came by here to get some info from the neighborhood newspaper.

You so stupid Skye. shit I hope for her sake she told her what she needed to know.

Me too, Skye.

Hello, Ms. Pat it's me Skye honey. You home?

Skye look, the door is ajar, get you thang out we're going in.

Ok, be careful, I'm right behind you girl.

Ms. Pat, you in here honey? I don't hear nothing T. The girls start walking towards the kitchen and even though their guns have flashlights on them, Skye couldn't believe what she was seeing.

OMG! T is that...

Yep, damn Ms. Pat! What the hell happened to her? I don't know.

When they looked at Ms. Pat she was sitting at her kitchen table and her head was face down on the table, blood was everywhere. The girls looked at each other in disbelief.

T, do you think my sister did this?

Let's get out of here Skye, we don't want to be implicated in any way. Walk backwards in the same steps you came in.

Ok, got it.

The girls exit the house and make it for the car. They both jumped in and pulled the fuck off. Skye and Tenika both think the same thing, Harper is on a rampage, she's gone rogue! The car ride was silent for about an hour before anyone said anything.

T, do you...

Yes, no doubt. It was her. It's kinda her signature. Harper has someone in her sights, we need to figure out who? And why? Before she finds them.

I agree T, but, do you believe that stuff she was talking about it being our sister Janelle behind this? I can't see it. I mean I know her and Janelle have always had this healthy competition thing going on since I can remember.

Well, that hasn't always been a healthy sibling rivalry. What do you mean?

Well, your sisters had one huge fight when they were younger and Harper vowed from that day on to never fight with her sister again.

What happened?

Harper beat her ass. Janelle never got over that I don't think, after twenty years you'd think she would be over all that old shit. But, some people carry grudges. So, to answer your question. Yes, I believe Harper believes her sister is behind all this.

We gotta find her T, I'm scared for them both. I can't lose my whole family man.

Tenika grabs Skye and holds her to try and console her.

She is crying uncontrollably right now.

Skye, I know you;re upset. But, you have got to shake that shit off, ok? We need to find your sister. Where would she go?

Think!!

Ok, ok, let's try her house in Castro Valley. She loves that house and that's where she can relax and brainstorm. And, not for nothing, it's a fuckin fortress, custom made fortress. Ok boo.

Ok, you got anything back from the feelers we sent out? Not yet, oh wait. I have a text.

From who?

It's one of my goons, chill. Let me call him, the text says I found your sister's car parked at the cemetery earlier tonight and there were a few other cars there too. Hey, just got your text. What did you see?

Just like I said before, her truck was parked near the mausoleum.

Ok. good work. Keep checking. Call me with an update ASAP!

Got you. One.

What did he say?

He said he saw Harper's truck parked at the cemetery where Mother and Janelle are buried. Why would she be there?

She probably needed to speak with your Mother about what's going on, I guarantee you Harper is hurt. And when she hurts, she goes to this very dark and violent place.

Ain't that the truth. Well let's go to the cemetery and just check it out.

Ok, let's do it.

The girls arrive at the cemetery and as soon as Skye got out of the car she felt some type of way. It was something in the air, she knew mayhem was coming! They proceeded to walk over to the Mausoleum to see mother and when they arrived they saw the plaque where Janelle's coffin laid, it was carved out and placed back. Marble chunks and small to medium rocks were scattered everywhere. T and Skye are standing there in disbelief, they can't figure out what Harper would want with our sister's body? This is getting way too deep and freaky.

What is she doing T? You know her the best between us.

I have no idea at this moment. I know she is mad as hell, I see that shit. Duh, bitch. She desecrated the place. Mother's place of rest.

Skye looks up to the sky holding her hands out up to the Lord asking him to protect me and to guide her to me. T had not seen her pray before, it was a good sight to see, knowing Sky thinks everything is funny. But, I know she knows how important and dangerous this situation is.

Let me think for a minute Skye, I'm sure I will be able to figure out Harp's next move.

Well, bitch walk and think. We need to get the fuck out of here before anyone comes and finds our uninformed asses here! Ok? Ok.

Ok fool, slow down and let my damn arm go. I got it. Alright, now what?

Drive. I need to think. As a matter of fact, call some folks and put off some feelers so we can get a lead on her. Someone might have seen her tonight.

Ok, that's a start.

Skye drives around town for about two hours while Tenika can come up with a plan on where Harp may be or go. Skye starts to get impatient, she's driving around and is beginning to feel like the help. She starts to think to herself, Harper what are you up to sister? And at that moment she realized that Bobby is a new recruit but has been up Harper's ass on trying to get promoted. Maybe he knew something. Skye knew that her sister wanted to do this on her own or whatever reason, and she is not gonna use anyone I know because she knows that I would get it out of their ass. Yeah that's it.

What's it? Says T looking at Skye like, what the hell are you over there mumbling about? Bobby bitch. I got to thinking. Harper is not gonna use anyone that I know or you for that matter because she knows we're coming right behind her no matter what she says, so I thought of Bobby Friedman. He started working for The Family about a year ago or so and he been up Harp's ass about getting promoted, that kind of do whatever a nigga need to do type of mothafucka.

You sure?

Bitch yes, think about it. She doesn't want us involved because whatever is going on, Harper has figured out something, in order for her to get all the facts, she's gonna need someone she can use, that obeys command well, and that has no loyalty to me or anyone else. Harper hired him herself as part of her personal detail. It's all starting to make sense now.

I agree with you Skye, that shit does make sense. You got a line on this nigga?

No, but I can find out.

Good, while you're doing that I'm gonna look through some of these papers we found at the kidnapping spot.

Why?

I don't know, I got a hunch, we missed something. Cool, anything and everything helps right now.

Skye continues to call her people to see if anyone has a line on this Bobby guy. As they are both in strategize mode, Tenika starts looking through the paperwork and photos of some girl that looks a little like Janelle. The receipts she picked up were for plastic surgery,

What the hell kind of plastic surgery was Janelle getting?

As she continued to read on, she also found a letter from a doctor in upper state New York, stating how he so appreciated the donation to his favorite charity in his name and the surgery was an amazing success. He hopes that he has satisfied her requests of him. T starts to think to herself, requests of him? What the hell is Janelle up to? So, T starts to look at some photos of the same girl but she now looks completely like Janelle. There are pictures of her hands, feet, thighs, legs, face, breast, everything. Up close photos too. Suddenly, it became clear. T couldn't believe what she was thinking, but what else could there be. She keeps this information away from Skye for now, just until she can be sure.

Meanwhile, the police get a call from the cemetery claiming vandalism and damages to some Crypts in the Mausoleum.

Hey Detective Mooreshak. Yeah chief.

I need you to go check out this complaint at the cemetery.

Are you serious Chief? There are uniformed police for that crap. I have homicides to solve.

Yeah save it! This is something you're gonna wanna hear once you find out who Crypt was desecrated?

Who's?

Here's the address, go do your job, and if you ever try to tell what your job is or how to do mine, your ass will find it in a uniform again! Now, get to work!

On it Chief, Sorry Boss. Ahhhh, get the hell out of here.

Detective Mooreshak has had a hard on for this family since Mother first started doing her own thang outside of The Family business. He's been a cop for thirty-four years. He could never catch mother red handed doing anything and it used to burn his ass, according to his words. Mother knew how to play the game. She used to be with my grandfather all the time when he was making all those deals for all the real estate my family owns, some deals didn't always go as smoothly as others. Some palms needed to be greased and greedy men demanded what they thought was their cut. So he made sure either he had something evenly crooked on them or they signed a contract, so the price could never go up, Ever! Grandfather was a shrewd businessman but he got what he wanted, finding how they play games, and play it better! That's simple. When Detective Mooreshak entered the property and saw the desecration of the Crypts, his little cop mind started turning.

Good evening officer, what do we have?

Well, nothing really, Ms. Janelle Diamond's Crypt was defaced and apparently taken out and then placed back in.

Anything missing officer?

Not that we can tell. Looks like some punk kid trying to pull a prank. Or maybe someone trying to earn some stripes or something, who the hell knows with these fools out here.

Yea, maybe you're right.

What are you thinking, Detective? Something more? Maybe, bag everything officer.

Will do Detective. Good, take care tonight.

As the Detective walks back to his car he is trying to figure out if this is some prank or much more, much more?

Mooreshak has always been suspicious of Mother. He would get close but when he thought he may have her on something, he got turned away. His thinking was corruption. He was right too. Mother had Politicians, Law Enforcement, Judges, on The Family payroll. Yet, his suspicions would fall on deaf ears. Noone at his precinct or higher up wanted to hear anything about Ms. Jackie Diamond. They would obviously be incriminating themselves, so Mother and her children had a sort of protective shield over us. Until people get greedy, well then accidents do happen everyday you know. Mooreshak looks at his watch and notices it's eight in the morning and the library is now open. He wanted to do some research on the deaths of the Diamonds. He always felt something just didn't sit right with him with either death, my Mother's or Janelle. He gets to the library and sits down at the newspaper section and begins to go to work. Looking for any discrepancy they may have missed. The crime scene photos are burned into his memory so he needs somewhere else to look.

Harper arrives at her other house in Pacifica. This palace overlooks the beautiful ocean and has panoramic views. Harper loves the ocean and windows so they are large and panoramic. She pulls into her garage and turns the car off. Sitting there she is just thinking about how she feels the hairs on the back of neck standing up, when Harper feels that it usually means something is coming. She starts taking off her clothes right there in the garage and throws everything into the washer. She enters the house completely naked and goes directly upstairs and straight into the bathroom. She draws her a bubble bath and goes into her closet inside her bedroom and grabs her most comfortable nightwear. She is suddenly so exhausted. She sees flashes of her and Julian's life, when it was good.

I can't believe I wanted to marry this fool. Harper thinks to herself, He betrayed me to the point of no return and I still have love in my heart for this disloyal, selfish, pathetic ass nigga. Disgusting! She retreats downstairs to the kitchen turning on lights as she goes around the house, she opens her wine fridge and grabs her favorite cabernet sauvignon a year of 1976, Red of course and pours her a very tall glass in her crystal glassware. Harper has eleven cameras in and around her house. The screens in the house, which are also in every room show each and every inch of her property. Each screen is fifty-five inches so the pictures are very clear. There are also motion cameras and lights around the home. When Harper starts pouring her glass of wine, she sees the backyard motion light come on, she checks the screen in the kitchen and she sees a big ass mountain lion crossing her enormous yard just passing through, they always do that.

Damn mountain lions, there are God's creatures too Harper. So, she pays it no mind and retreats back upstairs to catch her running bath water. Harper cannot wait to sink herself into that custom made, old Victorian deeply sunken tub with jacuzzi jets. She sets her glass of wine down neat to the bathtub on the glass table that sits next to it. She grabs a towel and something else and gets into her hot much needed bubble bath. As she sits and relaxes for the first time in what seems like forever. She feels the spirit of her Mother in the room. Harper was always sensitive to connecting to the other side since she was a little girl.

She turns on the camera screen in the bathroom and a couple of the other motion detector lights come on.

Come on lil guy, move and go about your way.

Harper says out loud speaking at the camera screens, thinking it's that damn lion again. Harper lays back putting a hot cloth over her eyes sinking further and further into that tub. As she sits a bit longer she glances over to the screen and sees Detective Mooreshak creeping around the property looking for a way to breach the security system. Harper sees him and proceeds to pick up the phone next to the bathtub which not only makes phone calls but can be used as a loudspeaker and in case of an emergency.

May I help you Detective? She scared the shit out of him. He damn near jumped out of his skin.

You can see me?

Of course I can see you. What can I do for you, I haven't seen your face in some time now.

You're absolutely right Harper. I was assigned to a case tonight and I thought you and I should talk. Is that possible?

Why would a case you're working make you want to talk to me?

There was a break in at the Mausoleum where your Mother and sister are buried.

Break in, you came all this way for a break in, that seems to warrant a phone call, don't you think?

Maybe, do you think I could come in and speak with you instead of yelling into this camera?

Sure Detective, come on in. The front door is open.

Harper has her whole house programmed and operated from one remote. So, she can unlock the doors and a plethora of other cool shit.

She knows he's up to something and he came here alone. Mother always told me not to trust him, he doesn't have our best interest at heart at all and would never take any payouts. As he enters the house he is amazed by the beautiful art and the decor is so not what he expected. Very sheik.

You're gonna need to come upstairs Detective.

So, he proceeds to walk upstairs and admire all the photos of so many Dignitaries, and awards given to Harper for Philanthropy and so many other things. He gets to the top of the stairs and Harper instructs him to go down the hall on his right and she is in the first room on your left. He follows instruction and walks into the bathroom and is blinded by the gold trimmings and white decor. He looks over at the tub and sees Harper laying in a pile of bubbles.

How can I help you on what sounds like vandalism?

I'm glad you asked that. I was just wondering who would have enough balls to do something so disrespectful to one if not the most important family outside the Mob.

Well, Detective, as I'm sure you're aware, people do some silly things when they think no one's looking.

Oh, so you think it was children, a prank?

I have no idea. I'm just hearing of this for the first time from you. So, why don't we cut the shit Detective. What are you really doing here? Because I help notice you came here alone and have yet to call for backup, or what I actually think is, your Boss doesn't even know you're here, does he? You're probably trying to earn some stripes yourself right? Everybody wants to be somebody. Harper says laughing.

She counts that he is twenty feet away from her so she is watching and waiting for him to make his move. Harper has been around a long time and seen it all, this looks like a Hit, with a side deal for himself.

I can see in your eyes that you're lying Detective Mooreshak.

Lying, what are you talking about? Why would I need to lie to you Ms. Diamond?

Well, in order for you to do what you came here to do, you tried to get some info out of me and solve a crime to boot.

So, if I got this straight, you think I came here to kill you? And, I'm also trying to solve a case as well. Double dipping I guess.

Yes, something like that.

He starts to move closer to her. He has already moved seven feet. Stop right there Detective I am not dressed here as you can see.

Oh I can see that. You're a little too smart for your own good Ms. Diamond. Tell me something I don't know!

I'm gonna need you to get out now! Ok, Detective, coming.

As she gets out she stands up and pulls her .45 pistol out from under the bubbles and shoots him directly in the head. He had no idea it was coming. Harper steps over his body into her bedroom to get dressed. She picks up her phone and places a call into the cleaner.

Hey, it's me. Come to my home in Pacifica. I need my floors done. Thank you. You'll find your payment in the envelope in the mailbox. Text me when you're done.

Got it. Goodbye.

Harper is dressed and ready for the day. She makes sure that she erases the camera footage of the cop being there at all that day. She then opens the garage and gets into the 2017 white Ferrari.

I haven't driven you in a while. What the hell.

Harper gets in her beautiful car looking like a million bucks with her all white Gucci suit on.

Harper is sitting in her car thinking about her Mother. She feels her spirit inside her. That scares Harper a little, I mean the girl is ruthless on her own but Mother was a whole other level. The things she has had to do in the last forty-eight hours or so, is making Harper feel more empowered than she already felt. She picks up her phone. All these missed calls and texts from her baby sister are pulling at her heartstrings but she has work to do and she cannot afford to lose the only one she can trust. Harper has been contemplating the arrival of T when she showed up. Now, don't get me wrong but, I haven't seen her in a few years, I mean we've shared a text here and there. Or an email or two. But, Harp knows she has to think three to four steps ahead of niggas, someone is out there with a plan in motion to take me out. And, you better know it, I already know who it is and I think I know how they did it too.

She is called Tenika. As the phone begins to ring Harper begins to drive down her driveway, she is blocked in by ten to fifteen cop cars pulling up to her house every which way. They surrounded her with their guns out and pointed directly at her. She sits casually with a smirk on her face. She looks at her phone, doesn't say a word. But, she can see that Yenika answered but didn't say a word. Funny right?? She hangs the phone up and lights a blunt while one these fools decides who's in charge and orders me to do something. Ha, this shit is comical, seriously!

Get out of the car Ms. Diamond with your hands up! Says the cop through the megaphone.

I can hear you sweetheart, you need not to shout.

Please, step away from your vehicle ma'am! Put your hands where I can see them!!

Next thing you know as Harper sits pretty in her beautiful car, a man approaches her. As he gets closer she realizes she recognizes him. He has been to many Gala's and Charity events held by Harper and others. He knocks on the window. Harper looks at him and rolls her window down.

Hello, Commissioner. What is this about? And, is it necessary? Well Ms. Diamond. They are charging you with murder. I told them

I would bring you in quietly and peacefully.

Commish, you call this shit quiet? I live in a very affluent neighborhood, and some of my neighbors are celebrities. Seriously, you could've just placed a call. Tell them to leave and we can talk. You know this is bullshit anyway. They just want to pin something on a

Diamond, ever since my Mother died, some of you have forgotten, who butters your bread!

Harper gave the police Commissioner the most evil look, he knew she meant business.

By the way Commissioner, how is little David doing in that very expensive private school he attends in, where was that?? Oh yes, Europe!!

Come on Harper. There is no need for threats.

Who's threatening? I simply asked you how your kids were, whom I have met on several occasions. Now, are you going to get these fools off my property? Or, do I have to?

Fine Harper. Come into the office this afternoon. I will be expecting you! smirk.

Don't you always!! She says to him as he drives off with that

Harper is thinking to herself about how as soon as she decides to call T's ass, the police show up about a murder? What? I know exactly what to do, you know me but, I know you too bitch!! Harper sings to herself. She knows where she needs to go next to get the next clue in the Labyrinth of shit that doesn't seem to make any sense except in the most sinister way. She drives onto the freeway heading toward the only thing in this world that Tenika loves, her father. She thinks I don't know she reconnected with this nigga like ten years ago. I keep tabs on all my loved ones, for a few reasons but, mostly for their safety and my own. I found out that he reached out to her for help with his house or something. Anyway, I have a line on him just in case I ever needed an Ace. I guess I do! Harper picks her phone and calls Ed Warren, T's father.

Hello, is this Mr. Warren?

Why yes it is. Who do I have the pleasure of speaking with?

Oh hi sir, my name is Harper. I'm a very good friend of your daughters, Tenika.

Oh, ok how are you sweetheart? Is everything alright?

Why yes it is sir, No worries at all. I just got off the phone with your daughter and she asked me if I can bring you the gift she got for you when we got back from vacation.

Oh, well isn't that nice. But, you don't have to go out of your way or nothing honey.

Oh no problem, I was coming this way already. So is it alright if I come now? I'm in your area at the moment.

Well sure. Do you have the address?

Yes sir, I sure do. I'll see you in about twenty minutes ok? Ok dear. Goodbye.

Mr. Ed Warren suffers from Liver Cancer and he also had a stroke. The reason I know this is because T still uses the Bank account that I set up for her years ago. And when it was time for Chemo, who do you think she called? Right. My ass. This poor man doesn't even know I pay his medical bills. Anonymously of course. Harper arrives at Mr.

Warren's house. Lights on, good sign. She parks on the street and walks up the walk to the front door. Harper looks around for any animals or signs of anyone else that may live here. She rings the doorbell. Ding Dong!

Coming, coming. Who is it?

It's me Mr. Warren, Harper Diamond. Oh yes, come on in sweetheart.

The door opens and as Harper looks at him he looks just like her, or well she looks just like him rather.

Hello Sir. How are you?

I'm fine. You forget that sir stuff, Tenika says you guys are like sisters, come give PaPa a hug.

Oh my, umm ok. Damn.

Harper steps back, knowing older men all too well. Ok that's nice. Do you live here alone?

Yea, just me and my memories. Ever since the Mrs. died. Oh you were married. I'm so sorry. When did she pass?

Oh, sometime ago now. Have a seat, would you like something to drink?

Yes, that would be great. But, you sit down, I'll get it.

Thank you. The kitchen is right there to your left, that's really sweet of you.

No problem. Here open your gift. She got it when we went to the Caymans.

Do you like it? Harper yells from the kitchen as she's getting the drinks.

Oh my word, it's beautiful. It's a portrait of her.

Yes, she sat for three hours just so the guy could get every line and curve correct. I thought it was so sweet.

It is. I know just where to hang it too. I'm sure you do, Mr. Warren.

No, No. Call me Ed.

Ok Ed. Here is some tea for us. How many sugars for you? Oh none for me, the damn Diabetes, can't have any sugar, it could send me into a diabetic coma.

Oh well, let's get that away.

They both laugh and sip their tea. So, when's the last time you heard from T?

Oh umm let me see, that had to be the Friday before last.

Yep, right in the middle of Jeopardy. Ha, ha. That's how I remember, it was celebrity week.

Oh ok, I didn't know she had spoken to you when we were on the island. Interesting. When did she say she was coming home? Or did she say, you know how that wild child is.

Right, no, she came here a couple of days ago.

Really, you sure, a couple of days ago? I'm sure that was really nice for you.

Oh yea. I love when she visits.

Ed, do you mind if I leave her something in her room for her? It's a little surprise.

Well sure baby, you go right ahead.

Harper stands up and walks past him to get to the hallway and he's looking at every inch of me, nasty ass!

Thank you.

Harper goes into Ts room and begins to look for anything that would look like a clue. I swear if she has anything to do with this... Harper says to herself as she looks under the bed. There was a box.

She pulls it out and sits on the bed and opens it. All kinds of intel on me, my company's, my property's, pictures of me in all types of places. I thought T said she was on some island teaching some damn kids or trying to find herself or something?

Lying bitch! And just as she was about to close the box, she saw it, her proof. How could she? There is no way to get back from this. Ok, I got you bitch.

I got you!!!

Harper stands up and leaves the box on her bed open with all its contents sprawled across her bed. I want her to see this and know that I know now. I need to make my plans to include one more, nice. Harper walks out of the room leaving any thought of a friendship in that room. Whatever Harper thought about T, was wrong. She begins to walk down the hallway when she hears a car drive up the gravel driveway. Harper walks up to Ed, ok baby it was really great to see you again, I appreciate you letting me leave her something.

Ah, come on now, you're like my own daughter.

Oh, that is really nice of you Mr. Ed. Harper says, sharing a laugh with him.

Harper leans in to reach for the doorknob when as she pulls, someone is pushing in. Harper looked up and it was Det. Ryan. Oh my God, what are you doing here?

Oh Wow, Ms. Harper Diamond. What do I owe this pleasure?

Harper turns around and looks at over her shoulder with that, "whatever nigga" look. She politely walks over to ED and gives him a hug. It was so nice to see you again Mr. Ed.

Oh, yes it sure was, you don't stay away so long next time you are here? Yes sir, I won't. Did you need anything before I left?

No, I'm an old man, I need less and less as the days go on baby. Well, alright then. Take care. Tell T to call me when you see her. I sure will baby. You be good. Goodbye.

Goodbye Mr. Ed.

As Harper walks through the gravel dirt driveway, she hears footsteps behind her.

How can I help you Mr. Ryan oh, I mean Det. Ryan. she says sarcastically. Oh, you got jokes? He smiles really big at her as if she would be turned on by him.

What do you want, officer? How is the case going about my sister?

Oh, we're getting some leads, talking to some people. Ok, so... nothing. Great, keep up the good work officer.

Harper opens her car door and sits in the driver seat when she reaches for the door to close it, he stops her.

What can I do for you?

Harper, you know, I know what you're up to. Do you? And what is that?

He kneels down inside the door next to her and says, i'm working on it. As he looks her in her eyes, they stare at each other for a few and Harper says to him, How do you know Mr. Ed?

He's my father. Well, Stepfather. He and my mother divorced years ago, but he was always good to me. So I still come by to check on him from time to time.

So you know his daughter? Daughter? What do you mean?

Tenika, his daughter. You mean, you don't know her?

Oh, T. yeah of course. We met when our parents got married years ago, she's cool. A little weird but cool. Why? How do you know her?

Right, well good thing you're a cop. Find that out on your own. I will. As well as what you've been up to.

Whatever you think you got, bring it! Hard! Ok? Take care officer. Harper speeds out of the dirt driveway spewing a cloud of dust all around him. That was some good intel. Harper says to herself. She can't believe that her best friend is somehow involved with this big ass "takedown". The good thing is that T knows me, at least I think she does, because I surely do not know her any longer. Harper starts to replay her visit to Mr. Ed, T's father in her head. Still trying to wrap her head around the fact that Det. Ryan is T's stepbrother! What the fuck yo?? Harper begins to think about what she does know about Tenilka and what could be her end game?

Maybe Janelle and her band of disloyal thieves have recruited my so-called best friend? Anyway, they all know me and should know they better come correct or it's curtains for everybody!!

Harper speeds down the highway on her way to Mother's Mansion to do some recon work. Mother has everyone's backgrounds in her safe. The one I know about. Mother felt something was in the air before she died. At least, that's how she put it to me. I remember that day like it was yesterday. Mother and I were sitting in her office one day, and I heard what sounded like construction work being done in the backyard.

Mother, what are you doing to this house now?

Oh, Harp you know Mother has to stay three steps ahead! Just like I raised you three to be.

I know Mother, and you have. There was never a time where you disagreed with her, ok boo.

It just sounds like you're building another structure to add to the compound. Are you?

No sweetheart, come on. Bring your tea. Let Mother show you her newest idea.

Harper picks up her teacup as her Mother did and followed her out to the back of the main house. Harper was her Mother's best friend. It went without saying. They trusted each other to no end. They knew that each would keep the other's secrets and always be there, no questions asked, ever!

Look Harp, what do you think? Jackie says to her daughter with great accomplishment on her face.

Yes, you have drained the pool and looks like you're building something over near the pool house.

Yes, you're absolutely right baby. She says laughing. Wait, I know, you're probably wondering... what's Mother up to now?

Well, yes Mother, that is exactly what I was thinking. I knew you were. This is my latest find. My new safe. What? Where?

Right there, can't see it huh? That's the point. You see, you know Mother does not trust Banks, they steal your money. But, they are necessary.

What I am building back here is a safe underneath. Underneath what Mother?

The pool baby. Genius right?

Yes, it does have a certain James Bond kind of feel to it. I like it. So tell me all about what's happening.

At that very moment, Jackie and her oldest daughter shared their last secret before she was so untimely taken away. As Harper pulls into the driveway of the compound, she looks over at the key box and holds up her UV light flashlight to see if anyone has bees tampering with this box or tried to get in using the old keycode. Harper always sprayed a small amount of a fingerprint agent onto the keypad, so that when she holds her special flashlight up to it, she can see fingerprints on any of the keys. It also lets her know who, by the camera in the very middle of the box, looks like a screw, but it is actually, face recognition to entry and security camera. Harper gets a rush knowing little tricks her Mother taught her, especially when they turn up some intel.

Harper flashes the light up and down across the keypad and sees fingerprints. But, the prints were on the old code numbers. She grabs her gun out of her purse and enters the property, slowly she drives up and around as the driveway twists and turns around so many beautiful trees and foliage. Looking for anything out of place. Harper spent a great deal of time here so she knows it like the back of her hand. She approaches the front of the house and sees nothing. She gets out of her car and points her gun right in front of her and scans the property. Not seeing any threat, Harper walks up to the front door. She takes her keys out of her purse and puts the key in the lock. As she is turning the lock she has a memory pop up about when she and Mother were designing this place.

Yeah, it was all her vision. She didn't believe someone else designing where she would be residing. The cathedral ceilings to the grand piano in the main living room, the two hundred gallon tank full of sharks, with diamonds on the bottom of the tank for decor, not plain rocks. This compound holds twelve bedrooms and seven bathrooms with two olympic size swimming pools. A jacuzzi tub and gazebo. A restaurant style kitchen with a full time chef of course. Game room downstairs is equipped with every relevant game known to man. And last but not least a library, an office and also a master bedroom at the very top on the third floor. It was the only room on the third floor. Mother includes an elevator that goes up all three floors but the one to her floor needs a key. James Bond, told you. Harper gets in the house and after going down memory lane she heads straight to the pool house. No need to bring a bathing suit, Mother always kept at least ten Gucci and louie swimsuits hanging in the closet. Harper grabs her size and opens the door to the office inside of the pool house.

She opens the top drawer on the left side and pulls it out halfway, then she pulls out the bottom drawer on the right side of the desk halfway, she hears a click.

That's what I want, baby. Harper yells to herself.

She bent down to look under the desk and there it was, the little box that popped out. Inside was the remote to the safe under the pool. Inside that safe Harper knew she would find the answers she so sought. As she walks out of the pool house towards the pool, she hears something in the bushes.

What the fuck? Great you would come at me when you think I am unarmed, wouldn't you. Harper thought to herself as she slowly got in the pool, trying hard as hell not to make any splashes. She's in, she looks around to see if she sees anything. She peaks up from the side of the pool and doesn't see anything.

Dammit, let me get my black ass outta here yo.

She swims to the middle of the pool and dives down to the bottom, hits the remote and steps into a sliding concrete door. This corridor led down about ten feet and then turned left. Harper walks up the tiny hill to the safe room. People always said how much they all loved Mother's pool waterfall. Oh, people would gawk at it all day at some of our events, not knowing that the waterfall it's constantly pouring water in because when she needed to get into the safe or because of how it had to be built, water would escape from the pool as you enter the cavern and return to the waterfall like a beautiful whirlpool. So no water ever got out, nor did it cause any disruption in the flow of the water. Harper gets the key from around her neck and opens the door, it was kinda creepy down there in the dark. It's just a small lamp right near the door. When she was in she locked the door behind her and began looking for her answers.

This place was like a damp office under the sea. Or, at least that's what it felt like. I'm the only other Diamond that's ever been down here other than Mother. My mother trusted no one, I understand all too well why now. As Harper opens the safe and grabs the file marked Tenika and her father. She reads all the intel Mother has on her father Ed, it's crazy. This fool was a cop.

What the hell? That's got to be the connection between T and Janelle. An old ass cop with connections to his old contacts could be dangerous.

Harper continues to read on,

What in the world, it seems that T father Ed was not just any old cop, he used to be one of the first who started working for Mother. It says here that Ed was a distinguished detective for thirty years when he was asked to retire early due to injury. Apparently, he tried Mother in a drug deal gone bad. Harper looks further and sees it, it's right there in black and white, staring right at her. Mother shot him in self defense and after the shooting and everything, she had her goons approach him at his home and gave him the opportunity, he accepted with great appreciation. Even though he acted like she was the second coming when Mother offered him the job, she still did not trust him so he and his family were constantly watched.

The thing looking Harper in the face, those two little sentences are about to start a war!

No wonder this bitch has been MIA, T ass been in prison in South America? What the fuck is this shit? Why did she lie to me? Harper then began to look for the folder with all the names of every person that worked for her or who was on the take. She scrolled down the page and she sees his fuckin name.

I knew he smelled like bitch when I met him. Harper says to herself.

How the hell did I miss that? It seems like young detective Ryan has always worked for Mother. This mothafucka acted like he knew nothing other than what he heard about us, but no, he knows so much more. Him and his fuckin step daddy. That's ok, Harper always has a plan. She says to herself as she grabs the paperwork she needs and leaves out of the underwater office and goes back down the corridor and swims back up to the house. She goes into the pool house and is startled by good ole detective Ryan.

Oh shit, boy you scared me. How did you get in here? And, what are you doing here? Harper asks him as she drops her towel and sees him drooling and begins to get dressed. She can see him looking her up and down fantasizing about her on his face.

I'll ask the questions here. What are you doing here? He says to her trying not to show her how much he wanted her at that very moment. The amount of passion and ecstasy he can give her. His dick got hard instantly.

Excuse me, this is my house. Which is why I asked you that question? I heard you. He says, with his hand in front of his pants.

Yeah, but you have yet to answer my brotha. Harper says with a smile. I followed you, I have never seen you visit my father before, got me thinking.

Thinking about what?

Well in all the years I've been coming to see my father, I have yet to see Ms. Harper Diamond grace our home. Now, I've always heard stories but, nothing like the real thing and

about you and how beautiful you are, he says as he walks up to her slowly trying to play with her hair, looking Harper directly in her hazel eyes.

Excuse me officer, keep thy hands to one self um k? all right now. What do you want to know? Ask your questions, you're here now.

Why thank you Ms. Diamond. I will do that.

Good, take a seat, if you like. I'm just gonna step in the other room so I can put on some underwear and grab a sweatsuit real quick. Ask away, I can hear just fine.

Ok, well. Why were you there today?

I just recently saw my best friend, his daughter Tenika and we went on a vacation and she left early. I tried to reach her, but I couldn't so I went to the only person I know she trusts, her father.

Did he help you at all with that?

Not really, he said he hadn't heard from her. Harper says to him hearing the click of him putting one in the chamber. She grabs her gloc out of a drawer in the office and stands behind the door.

Oh, well maybe your friend will contact you soon. He told me she called him from the Cayman's and told him she was in trouble and needed to come home and fix something.

Really, what does she mean? Fix what?

Well Ms. Diamond I was hoping you could help me with that.

Harper knew she never mentioned the Islands or where they were to him or Ed. as she figured, they are a part of this. So, Harper plays it cool, sticks the gun behind her back and starts to come out but before she does, she looks through the crack in the door, officer Ryan has his gun pointed right at the door, so to hit her in the head right as she were to come out of that office. Harper pulls her gloc and aims it through the opening in the door and pulls the trigger. Right in the forehead, on his ass, he never even saw it coming. He just stood there with his eyes straight ahead and then he just sat down on the couch. Harper comes out looking at him and walks over to him looking him straight in his face and says to him.

I knew we would be here one day. When we first met, Harper whispered in his ear and said, I could smell bitch all over you that day.

She stands up in front of him and proceeds to also tell him

Oh, don't worry about Mr. Ed, he will be taken wonderful care of. Don't worry detective.

Harper can see his chest still moving up and down a little so she knew he was still with her, she took the opportunity to show him something.

Look detective, I have something to show you.

Harper puts a laptop in front of him and shows him the live feed of his step father Mr. Ed's house.

Do you see your daddy Detective? He looks so comfortable sitting there watching television. You know, he just loves Jeopardy. She hears some gurgling.

Now, keep up your strength now, you don't wanna miss this. You see, I saw your picture in his house on the mantle, mixed in with the others, you were smaller then but, I never forget a face. so, when I asked to go to the restroom, I left a gift.

Look!!

Detective Ryan took his last breath when he saw his father's house blow up right in front of him. Harper looks at him on the couch dead as a doornail and a single tear streaming down his face. She closes the laptop and closes Detective Ryan's eyes.

Goodbye officer, you should've stayed out of family business!!

Harper turns around with nothing but satisfaction in her heart. She leaves the pool house, leaving poor Detective Ryan with his thoughts. She walks into the house to get dressed. Harper decided to drive her Mother's Maserati today. It's one of her most beautiful cars. Cocaine white with custom gucci interior. She enters her bedroom and grabs her Gucci suit out of her closet with them red bottoms, them bloody shoes! After a luxurious shower, she turns on the news to see if there is any buzz.

Nothing so far on Ms. Pat or anything else she's done. I guess the right hands got greased this time. Greedy muthafuckas, but, it pays the cost to be the Boss!! That I understand all too well. Harper walks into the garage and pulls the cover off of the car. She sees her Mother sitting in the driver seat, on the phone making millions. Running shit. For real. Harper pushes the remote and opens the garage. She slips onto the supple leather and takes in the smell of a mix of a new car and her mother's expensive perfume. As she puts her purse on the passenger seat, she sees the silver box with her name on it from her Mother. She stared at it wondering what in the hell would Mother have for me now? Harper regains focus and starts the car backing out into the front of the main house. She picks up her phone and calls the cleaner.

Hey, I need you to come and do the floors and remove some furniture from Mother's compound   .

No problem Boss. Be there in twenty minutes.

Great, I have to go, so the envelope will be in the mailbox. Thanks again. No worries Boss. be careful.

Always my man. Always.

The cleaner has the only key to one mailbox on all our properties. It's not a mailbox that is sitting outside the house just so as not to confuse the actual mailman. Only the cleaner and I have the keys. It makes everything run a lot smoother. Harper begins driving down the coast thinking of the next move when she decides to clean up some loose ends.

Hello.

Yes , what up Boss lady?

Yo, I'm gonna need you to cash those checks. Understand? Yes ma'am!

Is there a problem Bobby?

No ma'am. I'll get it done, I know someone.

Oh, you sweet inexperienced Bobby, you will not be contracting this one out. YOU will cash all five checks or you're out of a job. Simple.

I understand.

Good I thought you might. I will call you at 6:00pm, to check and see how everything went. Ok?

Ys ma'am. Talk to you soon.

Good, don't disappoint me Bobby, I like you, but business is business. You got me? Yes ma'am. Understood!!

Harper continues driving down the coast and suddenly, she remembers the silver box she grabbed out of the safe along with all the other paperwork she needed. She sees a rest stop and decides to pull over and see what is in the box, as Harper pulls the car in on that gravel road, making her briefly think of the problem she took care of earlier. Then she snapped out of it real quick and continued to focus on the task at hand. She pulls right at the edge so she can see the view of the ocean. The water always makes Harper feel calm and clears her head. She opens up her briefcase and pulls out the paperwork and the silver box addressed to me. She holds it up and turns it around and tries to figure out how this damn thing opens. Finally, a small opening, a key! Where is the damn key? When she feels the bottom she feels it, a skeleton like key.

Thanks Mother. You're always there aren't you? Harper says out loud as if to have a conversation with her Mother. Which Harper actually did a lot. It helps her drive and make decisions.

Harper opens the box. She immediately sees a letter addressed to her.

She reads it.

Dear Harper "My Eldest" Diamond,

If you're reading this, it means I am no longer with you three.I won't get into how much I want you to watch over your sister Skye. That one, whew! She's a good girl though. Just feisty, you know? Of course you do. My right hand baby. Always there when I need her. I also want you to watch out for your sister Janelle. You heard me right, I said Watch out for HER!! She's up to something that can divide the family forever. I always knew it would be you to take care of everything honey, right down to the letter. I need you to know, even though I may have never said it to you, I love you! And, I have so much faith in your ability to run this family and all businesses that are attached to it. I know it sounds like a lot. But, I know my girl got it. Now, about your sister, Janelle. I started seeing a change in her moves. Very secret about things, spending money and not talking to me about any of her endeavors. Business or otherwise. You know us girls talk about everything. She was different, so I began to watch her. When I saw her and Dante' hanging tighter than two peas, I got suspicious. Given the fact that Janelle never liked Dante'. Jealousy was on her back and she could not shake that shit. When you were gone to Atlanta to start and run your new school, you were away from the

family for about two years, we understood of course
baby, and I am so proud of you. I had a meeting with all
my staff and of course Janelle is there and I announced
that real smart business women get out while the going
is going great! The look on Janelle's face told me that,
I have taught you three enough that you know all the
rules to the game, and if there is an obstacle in your
way, you move it! After the meeting, my goons told me
different things she was doing, buying up properties
with no names on the front. I started to think she
was getting high, so I had her tested. She passed, but
now she is aware of me watching her. She and Dante'
became more distant and hard to reach at times. So
I fired both of them. They were mad to say the least,
but you know your Mother don't give a fuck!! I put two
ex cops on them and got a whole lot of intel on both
of them. Dante' was starting his own group with a
youngster named Bobby something, I think Friedman.
I knew then that I would have to put my own down,
before they do me. Harper, I know my funeral is not the
way you wanted to come back home, but something
in me knew it would end this way. Tragically. By the
hands of someone close to me. They knew no way in
hell a stranger could ever get close to me or my girls.
But, convince an unloyal, thirsty ass muthafucka and
you got a recipe for takeover. Dante' has a twin brother.
He lives in South Carolina but I think he is here in
the Bay Area. I sent Dante' to Vegas to take care of
some routine business. I haven't seen him yet, that was
about a week ago, radio silence from him. Janelle left
on vacation for about three months, not telling anyone
where she was going. I finally tracked her ass down in
Beverly hills, Los Angeles. What the hell is this girl up
too? I want you to take everything I thought you and
what I have left you and put the unloyal dog down.
Remember what Mother used to say; "when you feed it

and make it part of your family, and it still bites you? Put it down. It will never respect you or be loyal. Well honey I know this is a lot to take in but, just know " A Diamond is made under the most immense amount of pressure, and they do not break! That is why we're strong and persevere in times of adversity!! I love you more than words can say. Tell my baby girl she is my most precious gem and to live life with longevity in mind.

With nothing but Love,
Your Mother,
Ms. Jackie Diamond.

Harper got out of the car to catch her breath. The letter caught her off guard to say the least. She begins to scream out into the open blue, falling down onto the sand facing the angry looking ocean. With its fast and huge rolling waves, crashing up against the rocks on the shoreline. Harper knows now without any doubt that she must find Dante' and Janelle. I did catch the name Mr. Bobby huh, trying to play me my nigga? Oh, I got you bitch!Don't worry. Harper gathers herself and gets back into the car. Pulling swerving, making a cloud of dust in her wake.

Harper has revenge on her heart. She heads down highway 1 getting her plan together. There is a lesson that needs to learned and, I do not mind teaching a nigga nothing!! Harper decides to call her sister Skye to see where she was. With her Mother's letter ringing in her head, she had nothing but malice in her heart.

She doesn't even see Janelle as a sister at this moment. The way they were taught by Mother, you never fuck family! And, if you do? You suffer the consequences! Period! She knows what's coming her way. Fuckin, disloyal ass bitch. I will kill her!!

Skye, where are you sis?

Hello, Harp is that you? Omg! Girl, I've been so worried about you. I'm fine honey, just tying up some loose ends.

So, I've been seeing bitch, what are you doing?

Skye, shut up! And listen to me very carefully. Where is Tenika?

She's in the gas station paying for the gas. Why? What's up and why do you sound so damn cryptic?

Listen, stupid-ass. T ain't cool. I need you to get away from her any way you can. Make up any excuse.

Why? What's up? That's folks right?

no, I just found out so much intel on this ho, she never was my friend. Fuckin 25 years gone down the drain. You can't trust her.

Omg! Harp. Ok, I know what I'll do. I got this.

You sure, I can't lose you Skye. you all I got left. Just… Don't worry Harp, I got it. I'll call you in about thirty minutes.

Ok, please be careful baby girl. I will, you too sis!

Oh, I will be just fine. Tell T, I want to meet her at the spot we used to play at when we were twelve years old. She'll know. Tell her I got some info and I need my best friend.

Got you.

I love you Harp!

Me too, baby. Talk to you soon. You better!

Bye!

Harper has something very special planned for little ole Ms.Tenika, so you think you can outsmart me, dumb bitches. I let shit happen around me, when I'm ready for it to stop, I stop it!! Now, let me go teach this ho a lesson in Loyalty!! Harper drives up to the spot where they used to play as kids. Good ole Diamond Park. in that nasty ass creek we used to love to walk through and play in. Wow, so many memories here. Harper pulls up, it's dark now, which is what she wanted. She sees some headlights pull up. Not sure who it is, she parks around the corner and walks in from the southside and on top of the hill where the big huge jungle gym stands.

T, gets back into the car and is ready to continue to look for Harper. Skye looks at her and says,

I just got off the phone with Harp.

What, about time. Where is her crazy ass? And, does she know about Ms. Pat? Really, girl you know she knows everything, shit used to freak me out as a child. I used to think, how the hell does Harper know what's going on everywhere around her? I swear she has a sixth sense. Bitch is a Genius. She has an IQ of 178.

She told me to go handle something and she wants you to meet her at the place y'all used to play as kids. She said you would know?? Do you know where she means T?

Yeah, actually I do. Ok, so I'll take you to your car. Take me to Janelle's house.

Are you sure you wanna be there by yourself?

Girl, anyway. Hell yeah that's my sister's house. Fuck yeah I want to be around her stuff right now. And, Harp wants me to get some paperwork from her safe. Oh, you know her safe combo?

Mind your business Ho, Bye.

Bye, crazy. Call me to let me know you cool.

Skye didn't respond to that request, she just got into her car and left. Part of her could hear the tone in her sister's voice. She knew that would be the last time she saw Tenika again. No one crosses Harper Diamond and lives to talk about it. Literally, no cliche'.

Harper sees T's car pull up. She has a perfect view from her vantage point of the hill in the middle of the park. She had been there now for thirty minutes, for Harper, that's plenty of time for her to scan the perimeter. T gets out of her car, looking for Harper. She decides to call her.

Hello, hey there best friend. Where are you?

I'm here at this park, at night girl. What's up? Skye said you found some more intel and she said you needed to meet me here. Why?

Walking over to the basketball courts, I'm sitting down on the benches Mother donated ten years ago, remember?

Yes I remember. Here I come.

Tenika knew something was up, but she couldn't think of what. It never occurred to her that Skye was trying to give her a hint but, when you think you're better than someone or smarter, you usually find yourself mistaken. T walks over to the courts and sees Harper sitting there, in the dark in an all white Gucci suit. Bad as hell. Bitch always could work a good suit.

What up bitch?

Nothing much, come have a glass of champagne with me boo.

Champagne, ooh. You must have gotten some real good intel. Well don't leave a bitch in suspense, what's up girl!!

Oh, let's toast, Harper says to her as she pours the five hundred dollar bottle of champagne into the two crystal flutes.

Toast to what?

Friendship. Cool, but, why here Harp?

Well, I got to thinking after I was cleaning up this awful mess my sister has caused.

Your sister, Skye?/

No fool, Janelle. She thinks she is smart, and she never really was. Mother and I carried her mostly. I mean, don't get me wrong. She has a couple of degrees, but as far as business savvy or having that Gene say qua!! She never had that. But, what can you do right? Family is family.

I feel you boo, family is family.

The two friends clink glasses and toast to their friendship. They began to talk about how they used to play at that park as kids. How many boys they met and got chased by. Good times man.

So Harp, really why are we at this park in the dead of night girl, talking over all our memories. You ok?

Yes, I could be better but, I'm fine now because I am now informed. And, you know how I love to be informed.

Girl, what are you talking about?

I'm gonna ask you one question and I would like the truth, we have been friends forever, I think I deserve at least that.

Sure, I will answer you truthfully, Harp. but, I am getting sick and tired of you always letting everyone know how smart you are. How you run shit. We know Harp. you forget as much as you know me, I know you. I figured by the way Skye was talking, she was trying to give me a half assed attempt at a hint to what you might want with me.

So, you came anyway, Why?

Because you're right about one thing, you do deserve something.

Ok, my question is, Are you working with my sister Janelle and Dante' to try to take over the family business?

You really want me to answer that?

No, I know the answer. Harper has had her hand on her gun since Tenika got out of her car. It's tucked right at the ankle of her boot, easy access.

Both ladies stand up. It was nice walking down memory lane with you Tenika. You've been a good friend, or at least you portrayed one real good. Harper laughs, she sees red and feels nothing at this point.

Harper turns the laptop she had sitting there toward her to give her one last gift. I want you to take a look at something I found. This is crazy girl. Look.

Harper pushes play and Tenika begins watching the footage. She realizes that it is her father at his home. First, she sees him speaking with harper then she sees it. Her face is in so much pain. She drops to her knees and begins crying uncontrollably.

Why? Harp? Why?

Now, T. you know the answer to that. You betrayed me.

Harper walks over to her old friend and squats down in front of her and puts her hand on her shoulder. Without any feelings left for her, she leans in and whispers in Tenika's ear...

You know better than anyone, what happens when I am betrayed T. and without missing a beat, Harper stands up and looks at her fucked up, so called friend as she lays on the ground crying and shoots T in the head twice at point blank range as she walks away. Tenika did not know that throughout the whole conversation, Harper was spraying lighter fluid all around where they were drinking and talking.

As Harper walks back toward her car she lights a blunt and tosses the lighter.

Everything goes up in a beautiful glow of gold and orange. Nothing left of Harper's scent to lead the cops her way. At least not until she gets to the main bitches!!

Harper gets in her car and drives to Giant Burgers and grabs a bite to eat. A lot to do, gotta keep my strength up. Harper says to herself as she eats one the best burgers ever made in her car. She calls Skye to let her know that she was ok.

Hey boo.

Damn, Harp. I was so worried about you.

Why? You know who I am. I get muthafuckas, they don't get me! I know that's right sis. Everything taken care of.

You know it. Where are you?

At Janelle's house. Looking for anything that could possibly lead us to these fools.

I have a lead actually. Dante' is in Connecticut of all places girl. And Janelle bitch ass is still on the move. But, she knows I'm closing in. I got Dante', so I'm halfway there, you know?

Right, I got you. So what's the next move Harp?

Well, road trip to the beautiful state of Connecticut. You down?

What? Uum, of course. Bitch you're not doing this without me. She's both of our sisters Harp. meaning she betrayed us both.

I hear you babygirl. Ok, get packed. And you know what that means. Sure do, no clothes. Just hardware.

You got it baby girl. Let's hit it!

The girls hit the road with rage and revenge in the sights. Harper drives over to Janelle's house to pick Skye up and on the way there Harper starts playing back the last couple of weeks and the wake of madness that she has left upon her city. She feels no pain! She understands that there is a level of respect that her Mother demanded and she intends on everyone knowing that, ain't shit changed!! That letter Harper found in the silver box in the underground safe. It bothered her. She had never really seen a vulnerable side of her Mother. But, the letter did give Harper a different feeling of responsibility. Harper always knew she would be leading this family in the devastated event of her Mother's untimely passing, which is what exactly happened to her. I guess Harper ust got the stamp of approval from Mother, one of the baddest bitches to ever do it!!!

Harp pulls up to the house and as she pulls into the driveway, she gets a feeling of nausea come over her. She had never felt anything like that before.

Plus, her mind has been focused on one thing, and that's REVENGE!! She gets out of the car and instantly she vomits in the bushes. Now, don't get it twisted. Harper Diamond is a lady, we do not vomit outside darling. Anyway, she walks into the house and sees her sister on the floor with thousands of folders and papers everywhere.

Skye, what the hell are you doing girl? You got shit everywhere. Harper says to her sister as she begins to laugh.

Girl, you will never guess all the fuckin shit Janelle has been up too. What?

Bitch, do you know that Ho sold her businesses to Dante'? What did you just say?

You heard me right. For the last five years Janelle and Dante' has been fucking and planning a full blown takeover. And, to top shit off... I think they set Mother up!! This game is cold, but Mother relied on Dante' to keep her safe. He was paid a hefty salary to protect her at every cost, his life even.

Do you really think that?

Yes, shit is just starting to add up. You know?

Well, I do. And, I agree sis. I went to one of Mother's many safe's and found some info about how she had been suspecting that something was going wrong in her camp. He had receipts and all kinds of evidence on these two and all the shit they thought they were doing on the side. I believe Mother was set up with that bogus meet and greet with a new connect on some expansion shit?

Really dante'? When they tried to tell me that shit at the funeral, I didn't bite them either. I've been on his helmet ever since. And, they killed her because they knew she was getting close. Mother was no fool.

You're so right Harp. you ok? You looking a little green baby?

Yeah, I think I ate something bad or something. I vomited outside girl. What? You never get sick sis.

I know right.

Ahh, maybe your ass is pregnant bitch?

Ha, ah you got jokes!! Let's get this stuff together.

Well, Harp I put the photos of all of us, over there. And, the paperwork surrounding mother's death. I broke this shit down to a timeline. We now know when and where everything took place.

Good Skye, that's smart. Besides I hate the fact that we were gone opening and running our businesses in other states thinking Janelle was holding Mother down. She will pay for this Skye! I mean that shit!

The girls start getting the evidence together and head for the door when on the way out, Skye spots a light coming from under a rug on the floor.

What is that?

What Skye? What do you see?

I don't know but, she reaches for her gun and aims it in front of her and says very softly.. I think someone is here Harper? When you hit the light when we were leaving, I could see a light coming from a slit in the floorboard.

Ok, don't worry. Harper says as she instructs her sister to be quiet by putting her finger on her lips. The ladies went to the best schools in the world growing up and speak five or six languages, sign language being one of them. Harper signs to her sister to aim at the floor, and find the entry point, she will check the perimeter. Harper goes out the back door looking for any way into the basement. Clearly someone is down there.

She hears noise in the bushes and then gunshots. Harper jumps over the bush next to the back porch and flies into the house calling for her sister.

Skye!! Skye baby where are you? Can you hear me? Says as she tries to see through the smoke in the house. The shots were glocks and twelve gauges. What the fuck is in the basement?

Skye??

Harper doesn't hear her sister at all. She can now see down through the floor and in between the smoke and silence she uses her senses to guide her. Harper took some training with the Navy Seals to learn how to fight if you suddenly rendered blind. She moves with stealth precision. Taking the broken stairs down. She realizes someone shot through the floor at us. Good, that means someone else to answer some questions. She walks down and sees her sister Skye lying unconscious in a corner under some debris. She immediately checks on her, she still has a pulse, good, it's weak though. I have to get you out of here sis.

Harper picks her sister up and carries her to the back out the way she came and put her in the car. She calls 911 and asks for an ambulance, hurry please.

Don't worry ma'am, I have dispatched rescue, the first responders are on route.

Thank you.

No worries ma'am, stay on the phone with me until they get there ok? Hello ma'am? Hello?

Harper could hear the fire truck and ambulance sirens, they were just the street over, she took that opportunity to leave and chase whoever ran out of there. There was a blood trail that led out and down the driveway. Stops at a buick old school. Harper looks in and the fool is still in there. She sees that it's one of Mother's old goons. Wow, really. She opens the door and he falls out onto the sidewalk.

Are you serious Russell, Mother took such good care of you. How could you?

I'm so sorry Harper, Janelle and dante' didn't really give me a choice. They told me they would kill my wife and kids Harper! What was I supposed to do?

After twenty years,you still don't know how to answer that Russell?

Leave me Harper, I'm hit anyway. Skye got off ten shots before the floor collapsed. Hit me in the side and chest. I know my time is up and I knew I would answer for this one day, I guess that's today.

Harper watches as he passes away. She takes his watch and wallet out to give to his Wife and Son. Then, she runs over and jumps into her car and burns rubber driving fast to get away from the cops. I have unfinished business to handle. Harper drove around for a while when she felt sick again. She stops at a gas station to fill up and picks up a pregnancy test just for the hell of it. She begins filling up her tank and she throws up again.

What the fuck man??

What is wrong with me? Damn, I do not have time for this right now God, not now.

Harper heads to the hospital after she goes and cleans up. They tell her that her sister is in stable condition but needs plenty of rest. I speak to the doctor in charge and let him know that my sister gets the best treatment and she will have an armed guard at all times!! Understand doctor?

Yes, ma'am I do. Please don't worry Ms. Diamond, we will take excellent care of your sister. You look like you could use some rest yourself, would you like to lay down in one of our rooms reserved for the families?

No doctor, I will be right back. Thank you for all your help. Make sure that you stay with her at all times, understood? Yes Boss.

Good, see you soon. Call me if any changes. Got you.

Alright, check you later.

With Skye in the ICU fighting for her life, I must find this bitch and extinguish hers!! Where would a rat hideout? Harper asks herself. As she begins to drive around to the old neighborhood, she sees a friend from back in the day. Dirty, what's wit it nigga?

Ah, shit nothing. How are you doing girl? You better get out of that whip and give me a hug.

You so crazy fool. How are you?

I'm good. I heard about your Mother, I am so sorry Harp. Thanks boo. It's been hard but, I'ma push through you know?

Right, right. You always do. Your Mother was always proud of you. And she knew you would be alright.

Speaking of that, Have you seen Dante' or Janelle around anywhere?

Actually, I haven't seen them, but I was talking to my homie earlier and everybody's talking about Dante' and janelle.

What do you mean, talking about them?

You know, the streets are talking babe. And, word on the street is, they are scandalous!! They are up to no good!! them two, ya heard me?

Yep, I love your damn country ass accent. Ooh, sexy! Ah shit girl, you know you can get it.

Yes, I sure do! Hey, do me a favor, holla at your boys and see if you can lock down a location on her. Appreciate it.

No doubt. Got you baby.

Cool, do you need anything? You know I got you on whatever? Yep, I'm good.

Alright, let me know. You got the number. You know I do.

Bet.

Harper now knows the streets are talking about the family feud. Nothing new, just don't wanna run these bitches off. Harper comes up with the idea that she will call a friend of the family and have them contact her about Mother's will. Harper picks up her phone and calls the person. She gave clear instructions and where to meet. I figure this need to all come to and end at the most obvious place, Mother's!!

Hello, Hi Mark, How are you and the family? Great. I need a favor from you, it's a little unorthodox but, what's new right? The two share a laugh.

Sure what can I do for you Harper?

I need you to meet me at Mother's mansion, now. The one in Oakland?

Yes, is that doable for you? Of course.

Look, I know it's late. I just really need your help Mark. I'll be right there.

Great, see you there in about twenty minutes. Thank you. No worries. Bye.

Harper drives to her house in Castro Valley real quick to pick up some hardware. Mother has an arsenal but I like my shit. She pulls in her garage and she notices her bedroom light on. The thing about harper's cars, they all have a quiet mode added to them. Except the muscle cars clearly. So, you wouldn't hear her coming. She walks in through the garage door which enters the home with her pistol in hand. Pointing it out infront of her, she sees the light go off. Well, no one knows her house better than her, so Harper steps back into her dining room and sits on a sofa loveseat she has set there. In that position you can't see her, but she can see you. Harper has had special training in four to five different defense skills. She takes her shoes off and moves along the floor with her gun in front of her and can see a person with a big build walking toward the door. Harper shoots the figure in the leg to bring them down. The figure came down hard, screaming in pain, Harper stood up and turned the light on in the room where the person fell, and from the scream she heard Dante's voice!!

Dante' Roads! How could you? You piece of shit. Harp, Harp, I…

Nigga, I know you don't think that wasn't rhetorical?

Harper has her gun pointed directly at his face. Her gloc and she does this beautiful dance, it's unbelievably, and more interesting, Dante' knows this. Kinda makes you wonder what he's thinking at this moment. Harper ties Dante' rat, punk ass up with some rope and shoots him in the other leg, to make sure he stays.

Now, stay. Like a good dog.

Harper starts moving like a fuckin ninja through her house. It was cleverly made for her in case a situation such as this one would ever arise. Wow, look at God. with keeping her back to the wall, she moves in every room looking for his accomplice. When she gets to her room, she doesn't find anyone. Harper ain't stupid, she knows this fool can't move without Janelle now, so where is she?

Harp walks back over to Dante',

Where is she? I'm only gonna ask that question once. Oww, oww shit man help me, I'm dying here fuck.

Do not waste my time or yours Dante', you know you're not leaving here.

Stop acting like we just met muthafucka. Where is she? Last time.

She's here. He said in a whisper.

What, I'm sorry I didn't hear you? What was that nigga? As Harper kicks him in the stomach.

She's here Harp!!

Harper raises up to stand and when she turns around she sees her. Pointing a sawed off shotgun at her. Now, they are at a standoff. Both sisters finally meet face to face. Harper starts the banter.

Comment vas -tu, ma soeur? Harper asks her sister in French. Harper didn't believe in making it easy for her. They have never really gotten along. Janelle has always been a jealous person who thinks her downfalls are someone else's fault. Bullshit. Their relationship has always been tumultuous. But, now it has turned deadly. With Fante' dying on the floor in the dining room, the two sisters were locked in on one another. An old school Mexican standoff.

Bien et toi?

Vous avez 'été' très occupé'. N'est - ce pas? Putain, rat deloyal!

Je sais ce que tu as fait, Janelle. Tu ne peux pas revenir, de ça nous savons tous les deux comment cela va finir!

It's good to know you haven't lost your whole mind. I can't believe you remember French.

Yes, there's a lot you don't know about me sis. I'm my own person now.

Apparently, for the last five years was it? I tell you how this is gonna go.

No, you listen. You are gonna let me and Dante' go, or Skye might not make it out of ICU tonight.

What? Your greed has no boundaries Janelle.

Both sisters are not taking a loss on this one. Harper will not allow Janelle to take anything else from this family. The two came closer together still with pistols in hand and pointed at each other's face.

Now what? Ms. Bosslady?

Well, this ends tonight and then I will fix things. Just like a Boss.

Dante' begins to yell in agony and Harper's phone starts

ringing. In the midst of all that the lights go back off and gunshots are discharged. Harper crawls down a crawl space she had custom made into a panic room. Right under the floor, you would never think anything was under there but concrete. As she slides in there, she answers the phone, Hey Mark. I know I was supposed to meet you but I just ran into some trouble. I will call you back when I rectify this situation.

Ok Harper. Are you ok? Do you need me?

No, I'm fine. Just family crap. Talk to you soon. Thank you.

Harper can see everything and every room in the home from the panic room. Janelle is still there but she is trying to help Dante'. This gives Harper a chance to slip out and run up on her, she puts her gun up against her sisters head.

You mean nothing to me any longer. You're a dog ass bitch, and I'm gonna walk you ho!!

Harps phone rings. What up?

The doctor needs to talk to you, it's not looking good Harp. get here man. Hurry.

I'm on my way. Bet.

One!

She grabs some of the same rope she tied Dante' punk ass up with and tied Janelle up to the pillar in her home. It's bolted to the floor. So, she'll be there when she gets back. Harper leaves for the Hospital like a bat out of hell! She arrives and pulls up to emergency. Threw her keys to the security guard and asked if he could park it please. She runs inside and finds Tank.

What happened?

I don't know Harp. I have been here for the entire time. I know Tank, I believe you. Where's the doctor?

Here he is.

Hello doctor, my name is, I know Ms. Diamond, your sister is in stable condition now. We had a little infection that gave her a fever. We are treating it with antibiotics and she should recover fine.

Thank you Dr. Yoshito.

No problem. Call me if you need anything else. Ok, thank you again sir, she's all I have left.

She'll be fine Ms. Diamond. Just go get some rest. We got her here. Ok doc.

Tank, I need to go take care of some unfinished business No problem BossLady. I got her. Don't worry.

Thank you baby.

As she walks out of the hospital, she asks the security guard where is my car sir?

Oh, right here. You got a great park close. You were lucky.

I ain't never felt lucky, but thanks. Have a good night. You too maam.

She starts to head for the house and when she approaches she strategizes first. She pulls up into the garage again. Close it and come around the backyard. She looks through her balcony window and sees no one, what the hell!! She says to herself.

Janelle and Dante' were both gone. How did he survive those wounds? How did she get herself free? Where is she now? All these questions need answers. Harper realizes that when she catches her next time, no words. Just justice. Harper Runs into her bathroom with an intense feeling to vomit. Aww fuck. What the hell man? She opens the drawer and grabs the pregnancy test. As she pees on the stick, she was wondering if this is something she may want? She waits for the two minutes to run out and she looks at the test and her heart drops. Which gave her mixed emotions.

What will Harper do now that her sister is back on the loose and is she really pregnant? Will Skye make it out of ICU? Harper knew she needed to get her house in order!! Quickly!! In respect for Mother, she must avenge her death as well as cleaning up this mess. Will she have enough ice on her heart to do what needs to be done?

THE END

ABOUT THE AUTHOR

My name is Vanetta Mason. I am an Intelligent, Inspiring African American Woman who is an Artist with a Gargantuan amount of Creativity. I am a Strong Woman who is the Single Mother of an Extraordinary young man named Theo. He is 26 years old and is the entire reason why I chase my dreams so vigorously. Without the Love and Guidance of my Lord and Savior Jesus Christ and the Love and Support of my Son and family I would not be the Incredible Woman I am today. I am a true believer that you can accomplish whatever you put your mind to as long as you believe in yourself! I always knew that I would become a Published Author. Writing has always been a passion of mine. I have been writing short stories, poems, songs, spoken word versus since I was in Junior high school. I am the eldest of three children. My two younger sisters Monica and Britney Mason are my best friends and have given me so much inspiration. This book is just the first installment of a series. I would like to make The Diamond Family an Amazing Franchise! I am extremely sure that you will enjoy this Extraordinary journey my works will take you on.